Camilla is an engineer turned writer after she quit her job to follow her husband in an adventure abroad.

She's a cat lover, coffee addict, and shoe hoarder. Besides writing, she loves reading—duh!—cooking, watching bad TV, and going to the movies—popcorn, please. She's a bit of a foodie, nothing too serious. A keen traveler, Camilla knows mosquitoes play a role in the ecosystem, and she doesn't want to starve all those frog princes out there, but she could really live without them.

You can find out more about her here: www.camillaisley.com and by following her on Twitter.

@camillaisley
www.facebook.com/camillaisley

Also by Camilla Isley

Romantic Comedies

Stand Alones

I Wish for You

A Sudden Crush

First Comes Love Series

Love Connection

I Have Never

A Christmas Date

To the Stars and Back

New Adult College Romance

Just Friends Series

Let’s Be Just Friends

Friend Zone

My Best Friend's Boyfriend

I Don’t Want To Be Friends

FRIEND ZONE

JUST FRIENDS BOOK 2

CAMILLA ISLEY

This is a work of fiction. Names, characters, businesses, places, events and incidents either are products of the author's imagination or are used fictitiously. Any resemblance to actual events or locales or persons, living or dead, is entirely coincidental.

ISBN: 1542655862
ISBN-13: 978-1542655866

Dedication

To all friends who are in love with each other…

One

Rose

Now

Inside the Smithson's country house, Rose followed Ethan up the stairs and down a corridor with too many white doors to count. He stopped in front of one toward the end, pausing with his hand on the handle. "You're about to have a glimpse into my teenage lifestyle," he said, and flung open the door.

Sprawled on Ethan's bed was a bulging middle-aged man, fast asleep and snoring.

"Rose, meet Uncle Frank." Ethan sighed. "He must've decided my room was as good a place as any to fall asleep."

Rose giggled, taking in what she could of Ethan's room before he closed the door. As it clicked shut, they tiptoed away, careful not to wake the sleeping man.

"We'll have to take one of the guest rooms." Ethan turned on his heel and headed back toward the beginning of the hall.

He opened a random door. Before Rose could peek inside, Ethan roared and rushed into the room. Rose made to follow him but stopped dead on the threshold. She raised a hand to cover her mouth as she stared at the scene before her eyes in shocked silence…

Two

Alice

Seven Months Ago

Jack had beaten her to the library. He was waiting inside the small reading room, head bent over his laptop, and a cute frown on his face. He hadn't spotted her yet, so Alice paused and studied him through the glass door.

Even seated, it was easy to tell Jack was tall; all basketball players had to be. Not to mention playing varsity sports gave him a lean, flat-muscled body all too visible under his tight t-shirt and faded jeans. Dark eyes and hair, high cheekbones, and a straight nose made her best friend dangerously gorgeous. And his mouth… it was made to keep girls awake at night, which unfortunately it did—*too often.*

As Alice leaned closer to the glass, a dark lock slipped out from behind her ear, startling her. She still wasn't used to being a brunette. What would Jack say? Would he like it? Only one way to find out. Alice grasped the door handle and her chest tightened. He would reject her. Telling Jack the truth now was a bad idea; she should wait. *Yeah, definitely wait.* Today was a regular work-on-your-group-project-and-not-tell-Jack-you-love-him kind of day.

Alice pushed the door open. "Hey," she greeted Jack.

"Hey, Ice." Jack looked up from behind his laptop. "Whoa!" His dark eyes widened in shock, and his gaze made Alice's stomach flip. "What's up with the hair?"

"Change of style." She dropped her messenger bag on the floor and sat in the chair next to him. "Ethan dumped me." Alice pretended the news was trivial as she set up her laptop on the table.

"So you dyed your hair black?" Jack tousled his fringe, perplexed.

It was a habit of his, one that made Alice want to run a hand through his soft curls every time he messed them around. The gesture exposed more of his biceps, too, making Alice wonder what kissing him would feel like if she were free to lock one hand in Jack's hair, pull his lips to hers, and wrap the other hand around the marble-like smoothness of his arm.

She mentally slapped away her hands, and said, "I was tired of the fake blonde. Like it?" Alice hoped the makeover would stir something in Jack, but he ignored her question point blank.

"What happened with the dude? You've been dating him for what… three, four months now?"

"Remember when I told you about the night of Georgiana's birthday party?"

"Your former sorority big sister?"

"A big sister is for life, even if she graduates and moves on to grad school. But, yes, her."

"She's hot." Jack smirked. "You should introduce me."

"Can't do. She's in Paris with her boyfriend until next semester." Alice rolled her eyes, and Jack laughed.

"So? What does Georgiana have to do with Ethan dumping you?"

"Well, he's her brother, for one—"

"Seriously?" Jack made a mind-blown gesture.

"Yeah. We were at that hip sushi restaurant downtown for Georgiana's birthday and Ethan ditched me at the table to go flirt with this other girl. But then he showed up at my place later and apologized, and I thought we were okay. It was business as usual—and then he ghosted me for a month straight."

"That's awful."

Jack was clearly trying and failing to keep his lips from twitching. Ghosting was his favorite breakup strategy.

Alice ignored his distracting lips, and said, "The radio silence was driving me mad, so last night I confronted him. He didn't even try to deny it."

"The ghosting part, or that he's seeing someone else?"

"Either. Both," Alice admitted. "At least he was honest."

"Do we know *the other woman?*"

"No, but she's a grad student, too."

"Hot?"

"Yeah, she's hot." Alice swatted him playfully. "You're not helping…"

Jack waggled his eyebrows. "Want me to seduce her for you?"

Yeah. Just what I need. "I doubt she's into college juniors."

"You never know," Jack said, focusing on his laptop screen. With a few clicks of the mouse, he opened the 3D model of a complex molecule they had to design for their

Organic Chemistry group assignment. Jack started to rotate the model but stopped to regard Alice with a suspicious air. "Wait, is this girl… What's her name?"

"Rose."

"How sweet," Jack said. "Is she a brunette?"

Alice's cheeks burned. "Yep."

"Hence the hair change?"

"No. Ethan made it clear I got a one-way ticket to the dumpster. Dark brown is actually my natural hair color. I've decided I want to be truer to myself from now on. Starting with my hair, I guess." *And my feelings for you.*

"If it's any consolation"—Jack knocked twice on the table—"Lori and I are over, too."

Alice shifted in her chair as a slow melting sensation started in her stomach. Jack's low voice did weird things to her. Especially when he was saying he was single. Alice had feared Lori would become a long-term problem. And now, *poof,* she was gone. Was it a sign she should talk to Jack today? And say what, I love you? *Nah.* Maybe a physical approach would be better with Jack. She should just grab his face and kiss that mouth. *How would he react if I did?* The thought made her cheeks flame red, and Alice decided to take it slow. She didn't have to kiss him right now. Better to hear about the breakup first.

Alice pursed her lips, schooling her face to appear concerned instead of elated as she spoke. "Why? I thought your bio concentration was a keeper, what with all her talk of med school and her short skirts."

Jack snorted. "Until she went from super fun to a clingy nightmare in the space of five dates."

"I wasn't the only one who had a bad night, huh?" Alice suppressed a satisfied smile. Her plan to make a move on Jack had just become much simpler.

"Mine was horrible, trust me."

"Worse than mine? At least you did the dumping." Jack hated confrontations, in particular with the girls he dated. Hence the ghosting. "What happened? Lori a crier?"

Jack scowled at her. "It's not funny. She's a kidnapper. Batshit crazy."

"A kidnapper?" That was a new one. "What did she do?" Alice was genuinely curious at this point.

"She picked me up after school because we had a date." Jack abandoned the 3D model and turned toward Alice. "So I naively got into her car."

"Wait—to dump her?"

"Yeah, my plan was to tell her and leave."

"Wow, no ghosting?"

"Nah." He shook his head. "I'd run into her too often to pull that off. She's taking pre-med Chemistry, remember?"

"No, I'd forgotten," Alice lied, and gestured for him to keep talking.

"So I got into her car and she drove away. I asked her if we could go talk somewhere quiet, and she told me I'd just read her mind."

"She was expecting the 'Sayonara' speech?"

"No way. This is where my tale gets interesting." Jack grimaced as if in pain. "I noticed she was heading out of town toward the middle of nowhere, so I asked her where we were going. 'A special place,' she told me."

"Oh gosh." Alice put a hand to her head. "This story is about to get dreadful, isn't it?"

"In a second. The best part is coming." Jack winced. "I tried to tell her I didn't have much time, and that we needed to talk. She ignored me and kept driving, insisting I had to see this place, no matter how many times I asked her to pull over."

"But couldn't you have made it clear you didn't want to go?"

"Believe me, I did. At that point, I had two options: either keep sitting in the car or grab the wheel and make her pull over by force." Jack frowned at the memory. "Lori literally kidnapped me."

"How long were you in the car?"

"Close to an hour?"

Alice let out a low whistle. "Where to?"

"Here's the best part." Jack groaned. "She took me to this scenic viewpoint on top of a hill and timed it so we would get there at sunset."

Alice almost felt sorry for Lori, except that her total fiasco served Alice's cause too well.

"My day is improving," she said. "Now I can cross myself off the most-humiliated-girl spot. What happened when she stopped the car?"

"I tried to speak first, but she wouldn't let me."

"Of course not." Alice chuckled. "What did she say?"

"She told me she was falling for me, that I was the only guy she'd cared about in a while..." Jack paused. "Her speech ended with the L-word."

"Oh gosh, poor girl. And that's when you told her?"

"Yep."

"And what did she do?"

"Let me just say the one-hour drive back to the city was… *awkward.*" Jack sing-songed "awkward."

"Well, at least she didn't leave you stranded on the hilltop." Alice's mouth trembled with the effort of not smiling. "I would have."

"Nah, Lori might still hope she can change my mind."

Alice's pulse sped up as she asked, "Can she?"

"No way. If I had any doubts, yesterday's trip cleared them up for good." Jack made a gun with his fingers and shot himself in the head. "Worst Friday night of my life."

"Really?" Alice couldn't hide her amusement.

He nodded. "Really. Ice, why don't you turn on your laptop so we can get going. You can give me more grief later. Deal?" Jack added a stomach-flipping wink.

"Deal," Alice whispered, suddenly out of breath.

As she powered on her Mac, her fingers prickled. Both their relationships had ended on the same day; it had to mean something. Today *was* tell-your-best-friend-you-love-him day. She'd wait until they were done with the project to speak to Jack. *Or jump him.* He was single and wouldn't stay so for long; this was her moment. After all, how bad could it go? Not as tragic as with Lori. The worst he could say was no…

Three

Alice

Alice burst into her three-bedroom apartment, slamming the door shut behind her. Ignoring her roommates' questioning faces, she crossed the entrance hall to her room and flung herself onto the twin bed. Alice hid her head under the pillow and suffocated a scream with the bedcover.

Both of her roommates followed her into the room.

"Are you okay?" Haley asked.

"Hey, what's up?" Madison said.

Alice rolled over on the bed so she lay facing the ceiling. Still holding the pillow over her face, she muttered something incomprehensible.

The mattress dipped as her friends sat next to her one on each side of the bed. "You might have to repeat that without the pillow covering your mouth," Haley suggested, her voice coming from the right.

Alice lifted the pillow to say, "I just humiliated myself in the worst possible way," and then hid her face again.

"How?" Haley asked.

She pressed the pillow harder against her face and shook her head, refusing to speak.

Haley tickled her sides. "Come on, out with it."

Alice thrashed in the bed, trying to make Haley stop. Finally, she tossed the pillow aside. "I surrender!" she yelled. "I'll tell you everything." She recovered the pillow from the floor catching sight of Blue, her pet bunny, hopping away from the commotion. Alice straightened and settled the pillow behind her head, then took a moment to study her friends.

On her left, Madison. An introverted poet in the body of a statuesque blonde who dressed like a boho hippie. Her long, soft curls were always loose, and a book was constantly in her hands, like now. On Alice's right, Haley. An edgy computer science geek with a sleek, dark bob and an urban style. Whenever Haley had something in her hands, it was some techie gadget with software in it. They were both smiling at her encouragingly.

"I hit on Jack!" Alice confessed.

Madison looked down at her with big eyes. "You didn't!" she yelped, her grip tightening on the hardback in her lap.

"I did."

"I take it it didn't go well," Haley said.

Alice groaned. "Worse."

"What happened to our plan of waiting for a gap in girlfriends while you moved out of the friend zone?" Haley asked.

Madison nodded, but kept silent; she was letting Haley run the interrogation.

"The gap presented itself sooner than we thought." Alice told them about the kidnapping debacle. "And you know how Jack is. He would've been dating someone else by Monday, so I… I…"

"Did something stupid and impulsive?" Haley offered.

Alice nodded.

"What did you do? Jump him?"

"I tried." Alice moaned with shame. "I threw myself at him, and he was like 'Thanks, but no thanks.'"

Anxiety broke on Haley's face. "I'm so sorry," she said.

"Me too," Madison added, looking fretful and worried.

Haley took Alice's limp hand, squeezing it. "Did he say why?"

"He said we're friends." Madison and Haley both kept silent, waiting for the rest. So Alice gave it to them. "And that's when I practically begged him for it. And he just kept saying no."

"You begged?" Haley repeated. "Give us specifics."

"He said I was his friend, and I countered by saying he's slept with all his female friends. He told me that's exactly why he doesn't have many left. So I told him Felicity is still his best friend, even though she's female, and he slept with her."

"Who's this Felicity?" Haley asked.

"She's his oldest friend from Indianapolis."

"What happened between them?" Madison asked.

"I don't know the specifics. Only that at some point they had a relationship that didn't end well. And Jack was all like"—Alice started talking in a mock dude voice—"*It took me two years to be friends with her again after we broke up. I won't screw up another friendship.*" She made a finishing gesture with her hands. "End of story."

"Hmm. What happened after that cozy little chat?" Haley asked.

"He told me I was upset about Ethan dumping me."

"Which is sort of true," Madison said. "I still can't believe my cousin broke up with you."

"It doesn't matter, really. I'm not upset about Ethan, I'm upset about Jack."

"How did you leave things?" Haley asked.

"I followed his lead and pleaded temporary 'I-was-dumped' insanity."

"Well, at least you didn't give him the 'I've been desperately in love with you for two years' speech," Haley said. "Harder to take back."

"No doubt," Alice agreed.

"What if Jack was right?" Madison asked. Alice flashed her an incendiary stare, so her friend hurried to explain. "I mean, he's not exactly boyfriend material, and you don't want to be friends with benefits."

"I know he's attracted to me—"

Haley scoffed. "He's attracted to every good-looking female."

"Fair enough, but we have a deeper bond. We're not just friends." Alice pointed a finger at them in turns. "You both said that."

"Yeah, okay," Haley conceded. "But put yourself in his shoes."

"How so?"

Haley sighed. "He's a guy, gorgeous, and he can have all the girls he likes. He enjoys his popularity with the ladies. When he gets tired, or when a relationship gets too serious, he moves on to another girl. But he has you for all his emotional needs. A constant, steady connection that he doesn't risk screwing up by sleeping with someone else. You told me yourself he doesn't have self-control when it comes to sex."

"Well, he does with me." Alice pouted.

Haley gave her an encouraging smile. "Which, in a twisted way, tells you how much he cares about you."

"He can keep Felicity as his emotional backup."

"Felicity is a thousand miles away," Haley pointed out. "You're here."

"And I don't think him confiding in his ex would work so great for you," Madison added. "Do you even know her?"

"I've seen her around campus a couple of times when she came to visit."

"Why don't you talk to her and get an informed opinion?" Madison suggested. "Ask her if it was worth risking their friendship for a shot at love."

Alice shrugged. "I don't have her number."

"Mm, helloooo?" Haley said. "Pity we don't live in a world where finding people on the Internet is just a name search away. I wish there was a website for that. How about we invent it and become gazillionaires?"

"I'm not friending her on Facebook," Alice replied stubbornly. "And I'm not talking to her. I can't risk anything getting back to Jack. I don't even know if I can trust her—what if she's still holding a torch for him? I'd pour my heart out to her, and the next second she'd spill everything to Jack. I'd be digging my own grave."

"You don't know that," Madison said. "Aren't you curious to talk to the only person who can tell you how the friend-girlfriend-friend cycle really is?"

"Even if she said being with him wasn't worth ruining their friendship, it would mean nothing. They may not have been able to make it work, but that doesn't mean it would go wrong with us, too."

"You want to be his girlfriend, and he doesn't want a girlfriend," Haley said flatly. "You could be headed down the same destructive path as Felicity if you're not careful."

"What if he broke up with Felicity because he wasn't in love with her?" Alice insisted.

"And he is with you?"

Alice shrugged. "There's a deep connection between us, something more than a friendship. If, as you said, he relies on me emotions-wise, what do you call that?"

Haley blew out, making her bangs balloon for a second. "Complicated."

"It is. But I'm tired of playing the 'friend' role, pretending I don't have feelings for him. I'd rather try and fail than not try because he's afraid it *could* fail."

"So what do we do now?" Madison asked.

Alice lifted up to a sitting position, lying back against the headboard. "We make him jealous."

"You were with my cousin for months, and Jack never showed signs of jealousy."

"Jack never saw me with Ethan," Alice said. "There's a big difference between knowing someone you like is dating someone else and seeing it with your own eyes."

Madison arched her brows. "So you're looking for a casual hook up?"

"Ew. No!" Alice grimaced. "I just want to show Jack what he's missing."

"How?" Haley asked.

"For once, I'll shed the geek uniform." Alice stuck to a conservative dress code in class, and Jack had never seen her dressed to impress. "It's time he realizes I'm a woman.

I could read indecision in his eyes before he said 'no.' He just needs a push."

Madison scratched her cheek before asking, "No chance you saw only what you wanted to see?"

"No, I'm positive, and I'm tired of pretending. I don't want to be his friend. Watching him sleep his way through campus is like dying a slow death. It makes me live in fear that one of his girls will eventually stick around, and she won't be me. I get anxious whenever he dates someone for more than a month, and I'm not interested in being his emotional fix forever." Alice waved one hand in the air dismissively. "If he really feels nothing for me, I'd rather find out now and move on with my life."

A muffled squeal came from under the bed. Alice bent over to reach and pick up Blue. "This is all your fault," she told the dark gray bunny as she stroked his soft fur. "If you hadn't scurried off to his room in our freshman year, I would've never met Jack."

A flashback of that day forced its way into Alice's mind.

***

Alice ran down the hall of her newly assigned freshmen dorm to find Blue. Her stupid roommate had let him out of his cage and then forgotten to close their door. Alice popped her head inside every room on both sides of the hall, asking, "Hi, have you seen a small bunny, dark gray fur?" But no luck.

Her anxiety grew with each passing door—until she reached the end of the corridor and stopped on the threshold of the last room. Inside, a guy sat on a twin bed holding Blue in his lap. He was wearing a simple white t-shirt, black basketball shorts, and man's slides.

And he was SO hot.

Alice barged into the room. "You found Blue," she shrieked, startling both human and bunny.

A pair of dark eyes focused on her and the boy's expression changed from slightly alarmed to interested. Something fluttered inside Alice's belly. Blue had stumbled upon the best-looking boy of the dorm: dark brown hair, square jaw, and a general tousled, bad-boy aura.

Alice lowered her gaze, suddenly self-conscious. His scrutiny felt like having a spotlight pointed at her face. She did a quick mental checklist of the state of her hair, makeup, and clothes. Um, probably not good; she'd run out of her room midway through her unpacking, in cozy clothes, no makeup, and her hair was a recently bleached mess.

"Hello stranger," the boy said, flashing her a mischievous grin.

"Hi." Alice pushed an unruly lock of hair behind her ear. "You have my bunny."

The hottie scratched Blue behind the ears, making him purr. I'd purr, too, if it were me, *she thought.*

"Blue, is it?" he asked.

"Yep."

The boy cocked his head toward her. "And you are?"

"Alice."

"I'm Jack."

"Nice to meet you." Alice took a tentative step forward. "Can I have him back?"

"Wait, don't I get a reward for finding him?" Jack teased.

He should get a reward for finding you, *Alice thought. Instead, she said, "Your reward would be that I take Blue back before he poops on you."* Did I really just say "poop" in front of a super-hot guy? *Alice blushed as she watched Jack's smile switch back from dashing to mildly worried. She closed the distance between them and took the struggling bunny from his hands. At the light brush of skin on skin, a shiver ran through her.*

"You start tomorrow?" Jack asked. "Or are you one of the luckies with no lectures on Monday?"

"Definitely not lucky." Alice shook her head. "My first class is at a stupid early hour."

"Same bad luck here. You pick a concentration already?"

Alice frowned. "Concentration?"

"It's the fancy word they use around here for major," Jack explained.

"Oh, that." Why can't they just call it a major? *"Chemistry."*

"No way, same as me." His face lit up. "You're in Professor Chase's class?"

"Yes." Same major—concentration, whatever—same classes. I'll see you almost every day. *Alice did a victory dance inside her head.*

"Me too." The "I'm interested" smirk was back on his face. "Want to go together?"

"Sure." Alice clutched Blue more tightly as the bunny tried to leap out of her grasp and back into Jack's lap. "I'm just a few doors down, room 254."

"I'll stop by tomorrow morning. Deal?"

"Deal."

"See you later, Ice."

Alice's face fell a little. "It's Alice."

"Mind if I go with Ice?"

Usually, her name got shortened to Ali or Ally. Lice once, thanks to a mean girl in fourth grade. But never Ice.

"Why Ice?" she asked.

"It has the most beautiful crystalline structure."

Oh! He was flirting with her using molecular structures. If this wasn't perfect chemistry...

Alice left the room and walked down the hall, but then, on impulse, decided to look back. Jack was leaning against his doorframe, smiling. He'd been watching her go.

***

"You would've met Jack in class the next day anyway," Haley said, bringing Alice back to present.

"Yeah, but if it wasn't for this little guy"—she kissed Blue and set him back on the floor—"we wouldn't have gone together. I wouldn't have sat next to him that day, or the next, and now I wouldn't be stuck in the stupid friend zone."

"It could be worse," Haley insisted. "You could've slept with Jack freshman year and now he wouldn't even remember your name."

On Alice's other side, Madison blushed a furious red. She was very self-conscious of one-night stands and guys ditching her afterward.

Alice crossed her arms and pouted. "Say what you like, I'm tired of waiting."

"What's your evil plan to make him jealous?" Madison asked.

"He's going out with the team tonight," Alice said. Jack played varsity basketball for the Harvard Crimson. "He doesn't know I know his plans."

Haley narrowed her eyes at her. "And how do you know?"

"A girl in my photography class is dating a guy on the team. She told me."

"And what are these plans?" Madison pressed.

"Halloween house party; I'm going, and you're coming with me."

"To a party populated by tall basketball players?" Madison smirked. "Who am I to complain? Where's the party? Is it walk-in, or do we need an invitation?"

"It's someone's house off campus, and all Kappa Kappa Gamma are invited."

Their sorority was where Alice, Haley, and Madison had met. After becoming close friends, they'd moved in together at the beginning of sophomore year. Greek life at Harvard wasn't residential, so no sorority house. Both Haley and Alice had been recruited as freshmen, while for Madison Smithson, being a Kappa Kappa Gamma was a family legacy. Just like going to Harvard, and then Harvard Law School. The sorority was also where Alice had met Madison's cousin who, at the time, was a senior and chose to mentor Alice. Now Georgiana was in law school. Weird how many people in Alice's life shared the same surname. Ethan, too, was a Smithson. The only one ever to quit the family's law firm to start his own real estate business. He was the black sheep of the family. *Alice, Ethan could be a golden sheep, you don't care. He dumped you! Stop thinking about that particular Smithson.*

"What about Emily's party?" Haley asked. "I told her we were going."

"Yeah, but her parties suck. We can stop on our way to say hello, stay half an hour, and then join the real paaarrrtyy." Alice bobbed her shoulders up and down to an imaginary tune.

"We're sold on the party switch." Haley nodded. "But just showing up won't be enough to mess with Jack. So...?"

"I've no idea. I figure I'll make it up as I go." Alice looked at her friends with a conspiratorial air. "Your task is to make me as hot as I can be in my costume." She struck a pin-up pose, pushing her chest forward and locking her hands behind her head. "I want to show him what he's saying 'no' to."

"All right, Miss Femme Fatale," Haley joked. "Let's make you irresistible.

Four

Jack

Jack was late. In less than an hour he had to be Halloween-ready, and he was still in the bathroom shaving. This was the last Saturday before the basketball season kicked off, a.k.a. the last game-free weekend for the next five months. To celebrate, the entire team was going to a house party. The address he had was just a few blocks off campus, meaning Jack could get as wasted as he liked with no car to drive.

And he *needed* to get wasted tonight.

What an awful weekend he'd had so far. First, a kidnapping followed by a traumatic breakup, and then his best friend tried to kiss him in the library. Women were crazy; he was past due for a guy's night.

No, not women plural, Jack corrected himself. One woman in particular.

He didn't care about Lori; she'd get over it. Ice, on the other hand... Dodging her once had been hard, but what if she tried again? He wasn't a saint, and her new look sorely tested his self-control. The dark hair was unsettling—*sexier,* even. Not what he was used to. And she'd tried to kiss him! *Don't think about it, Jack.* He'd mistaken his connection with a friend for something more once, hurting Felicity hard. The whole thing had been a disaster, one he wasn't going to repeat with Ice.

Even if it was impossible to forget the thrill he'd felt when she'd come close to him. How their lips had almost touched before he'd come to his senses and pushed her back—

Jack involuntarily jerked his head and cut himself with his razor. He threw the blade in the sink and washed the cut with fresh water. To stop the bleeding, he reached for a paper roll and pressed a sheet of paper on the small wound. This Ice business was affecting him way more than it should. She was just acting out because her boyfriend had ditched her. That was it. When girls dyed their hair and made a move on their best friends, they were acting out. It was nothing more. Ice would be back to normal as soon as she found someone else to date.

Jack frowned at himself in the mirror. All of a sudden, the thought of Ice dating someone else wasn't that pacifying. *What's wrong with me?* Jack had never had a problem with her dating other men. Then again, she'd never tried anything with him before. Since they'd met, he'd kept Ice locked in the friend zone. Okay, maybe not since day one. Jack remembered fondly the girl barging into his room looking for her bunny. She'd been impossibly cute with her messy blonde bun and worried frown. At once, Jack had vowed to make the human bunny his first college catch. But when they'd started seeing each other every day in class, they'd become friends. And now Ice wanted more. *Not going to happen.*

Ice wasn't the "friends with benefits" type—well, no girl was, really. No matter what they said, girls always ended up asking for more. Commitment, a serious relationship, *I love yous,* and all that. Jack wasn't interested in any of it. He was determined to enjoy his college years with no strings attached.

He removed the paper from his jaw. The bleeding had stopped, so he quickly finished shaving and rinsed the remaining gel from his face. The cold water was soothing on his skin, tempting him to dunk his entire head under the icy stream to cool off. One freezing shower apparently hadn't been enough to forget Alice had made a pass at him.

The doorbell rang, announcing Peter had arrived. *Good!* Peter Wells, his best wingman and team captain, was the fire Jack needed to melt his thoughts about Ice. If possible, Peter was even worse than Jack with girls. The Crimson captain was a senior and always dated a bunch of girls at the same time—freshmen to seniors, or even older. Exactly the bad influence Jack wanted tonight.

He dried his face with a towel, then wrapped it around his neck and went to open the door.

"Sullivan, my man," Peter greeted him.

They clasped hands and bumped chests, which resulted in Jack's hand getting smeared with bluish paint. The team had decided to go to the Halloween party dressed as Smurfs. The costume was very basic: white sports shorts, no clothes from the waist up, a white jersey beanie, and a *lot* of blue body paint.

Peter was wearing a team hoodie, for now, one the blue paint would make unusable. But the captain always wore team-branded clothes. His favorite pickup line was to tell the ladies he was joining the NBA after graduation. It wasn't necessarily a lie. Peter was bound to receive an offer from one of the big teams sooner or later. What the girls didn't realize was they'd be long forgotten by then. But just saying the three little magic letters—N B A—kept the WAG dream alive, and the girls fell right and left for Peter.

His blue eyes, dark hair, and impressive height certainly didn't hurt, too.

Peter gave him the once-over. "Yo, my man, you're late," he complained. "I need you to get blue and do my back. The lady doctor keeping you busy?"

"The lady doctor was fired," Jack said, closing the door behind his friend. It was another lady giving him pause.

"Already? What happened?"

"She drove me an hour out of the city to show me the beautiful sunset, tell me she loved me, and announce she was ready to move our relationship to the next level." Jack raised his hand sarcastically.

"Ouch!"

"Yeah, tell me about it. I had the worst night yesterday." *And the worst day, today. What the hell, Ice!* Jack shook his head.

Peter took his headshake for disappointment about the doctor. "Come on, my man," he said. "Tonight we're going to find you a hot nurse to replace the doctor and cure your soul. Now put on your white shorts and let's get blue."

***

The Smurf costumes were a rousing success. It was impossible for them to move around the party without being the center of attention. Twenty tall guys were hard to miss in a crowd already—paint them blue, and it became impossible. The ladies seemed to love the idea; the guys scored extra points for daring and originality.

Jack dodged a girl who was pushing through the crowd, sloshing her drink over anyone not fast enough to get out of her way. As she scurried by, Jack noticed the girl's face was smeared with blue paint. At least one of his teammates had already scored. Jack poured himself a beer from a huge keg and took position next to Peter in a corner that offered a strategic view of the house.

From his vantage point, he spotted a group of three girls with potential: a blonde and two brunettes. The ladies had their backs turned, but the rear view did not call for complaints. The blonde was dressed in a short, airy dress, which looked more like a babydoll shirt. She had little white wings strapped to her back. *An angel.* One brunette was clad in a tight, glittery black jumpsuit with only one shoulder strap. From her bottom sprouted a tail she'd laced around one wrist for support, and she had kitten ears. *Meow.* The last girl was wearing a short, sequined red dress and had tiny red horns on the top of her head. *Hell-o.* Jack had a good feeling about the trio.

He nudged Peter. "Angel, devil, or hellcat?"

The captain whistled. "I'll take the kitty catty."

A pang of disappointment stabbed Jack's chest; he would've chosen the kitten, too. Never mind. Angel or devil? As they scoped out their targets, a dude in an unoriginal vampire costume approached the girls and left a minute later with the she-devil. "I'll take the angel, then," Jack said.

"Let's see the faces first," Peter cautioned.

Jack stared as the angel spun around; she was pretty and looked familiar. Where had he seen her? Realization hit him a second before the black kitty turned around and they locked eyes. It was Ice.

Five
Alice

Alice turned her head and met a pair of dark eyes. She pursed her lips, trying not to smile. Jack was a Smurf—genius. His blue face was a mask of surprise—he obviously hadn't expected her to be here.

She whispered in Madison's ear, then dragged her roommate toward Jack and his fellow blue friend—from his impressive height, another basketball player—to say hello. Alice stopped in front of Jack and smiled. He blinked, stunned. He was gaping at her tight costume and not speaking.

"Hi," Alice said.

"Hi." Jack's jaw tensed and his eyes became wary. "Why are you here?"

It was time to let him know she could play *oh so cool.*

"Most Kappa Kappa Gammas came here tonight." Alice casually wrapped her hair to the side, leaving her bare shoulder and neck exposed. "At least, the cool gang did."

"My man," the blue friend butted into the conversation. "Aren't you going to introduce me?"

With all the blue paint covering him, Alice couldn't tell much about the second Smurf's looks. Just that he was super-tall, ripped, and had popping blue eyes.

"Peter, Alice," Jack said without enthusiasm. "Alice, Peter."

"Nice to meet you," Alice said. "I'd shake your hand, but I'm afraid of turning blue." She turned around to introduce Madison, but her roommate was already chatting with another Smurf. "How many Smurfs are there?"

"The entire team," Peter said.

"You play basketball with Jack?"

"Yeah, headed for the NBA next year, hopefully." He made a cute, no-biggies face.

Alice noticed Jack fidgeting uneasily at Peter mentioning the NBA. *Ah, the notorious NBA line.* Alice had heard of this guy: Peter Wells was Jack's preferred wingman, and the NBA reference was his favorite pickup line. Peter was hitting on her and Jack didn't like it. *Perfect!*

"The NBA, wow, how cool!" she said, playing along.

"Hi, Alice." Becky, a fellow Kappa Kappa Gamma dressed as a sexy nurse, stopped next to her. "Fraternizing with the Smurfs?"

"Becky, meet Jack, fellow Chemistry student and the only non-nerd guy in my class, and Peter, future NBA star," Alice introduced, trying to keep her eyes from wandering from their faces to their painted-but-still-very-visible six-packs.

"Hi," Becky said. "The house is full of Smurfs."

"Yep, the Crimson all came as Smurfs," Alice said. "So, whose idea was it?" she asked Peter.

"It was a team decision."

"It's brilliant," Becky said, openly staring at the generous amount of muscle on display.

"So, Becky, is it? My friend here"—Peter patted Jack on one shoulder—"needs some *nursing* back to life. He's recovering from an injured heart."

"Is he now?" Becky peered at Jack, then at Alice, as if she was silently asking, "Is he cool?"

The sultriness in Becky's voice made Alice's skin prickle with ugly emotions: irritation, jealousy, pain, and anger. But she disciplined her features, trying to appear neutral. If Becky ended up sleeping with Jack tonight, she'd be forgotten by morning. It was more important for Alice to act unconcerned.

"Jack's a darling," Alice said aloud, then leaned toward Becky to whisper in her ear, "If you're looking for a night's fun." She tilted her head and winked at Jack, then continued speaking to Becky in hushed tones. "Don't expect anything serious from him." The sisterly code of Kappa Kappa Gamma, and the more general girl code, demanded she warn Becky of what to expect.

The information didn't seem to bother Becky. She turned toward Jack once again, saying, "I'm out of juice." She shook the empty red cup she was holding. "Why don't we go get another drink?"

He chugged whatever was left of his beer and shrugged. "Sure."

As they walked away, Jack peered over his shoulder, catching Alice's eye. Confusion at her attitude was written all over his face. Then they were gone, and Alice was alone with Peter. Madison had disappeared with the other Smurf.

"You're a junior?" Peter asked.

"Yes. You?"

"Senior. And your concentration is Chemistry?"

"Yep."

"Whoa, tough. You're a smart girl, then."

"Were you hoping for dumb?"

"No." He shot her a grin, his teeth too white next to the blue lips. "I like a challenge."

"What's your major?"

"Econ. But hopefully, I won't need it—"

"Yeah, I know..." She waved him off. "Not with the NBA knocking on your door soon." Now that Jack was gone, she didn't have to pretend she cared about an alleged future career as a pro athlete.

"You're not into basketball?"

"Not a sports fan in general."

"Ouch."

"What? Did I ruin your best pickup line?" Alice smiled to soften the blow.

"Touché. Are you from around here?"

"No, I'm originally from Philly. You?"

"Florida. Small town near Orlando."

Alice studied him for a few seconds. "I'm trying to imagine your face without the blue paint."

"Careful with that, I'm told I'm devastatingly handsome."

"And modest, too."

"You really have no idea how I look? Haven't you been to a game? Not even once to see Jack play?"

"No. Jack knows I don't care about sports." He also didn't want her anywhere near his teammates, she suspected. "I don't even know the rules. I get you guys have to throw the ball inside the basket, but that's about it."

Peter chuckled. "I guess in the end that's all that really matters. You should give basketball a shot. It's a beautiful game." He winked. "If you want, I can explain the basics to you."

"It's too loud in here to concentrate on a game's rules."

"Rain check for tomorrow?"

Now he was playing a whole different ball game, but why not play along? If she really wanted to make Jack jealous, Peter would do the trick, and he might be a little treat for her self-esteem, too. She needed someone to look at her in a way that made her feel beautiful. Desirable. And Peter had definitely mastered that particular skill.

"How about you grab me a drink for now?" she asked.

"What are you having?"

"Beer."

"Wait here, I'll be right back."

Peter disappeared behind a corner and was back in a couple of minutes with two blue cups in his hands. He offered her one, saying, "Want to move upstairs? It's too noisy to talk down here."

Dangerous question.

"Sure," Alice said.

Dangerous answer.

She followed him up the stairs, half-curious, half-worried to see if he would try to take her into a room. But Peter stopped at the top of the stairs and sat on a carpeted step. Alice sat next to him, keeping a safe distance.

"I don't bite," he said.

"But you stain." She bumped her cup into his. "Cheers."

"To what?"

"To an evening with a blue guy." She raised her cup, and they both drank.

"Would you get terribly mad if I got some paint on you?"

Alice held his burning gaze. "It depends where."

He took the cup from her hands and set it alongside his on the landing. "How about on your lips?"

"You can try." She smiled. "I promise I'll keep my claws in."

Careful not to touch her in any other way, he leaned in and pressed his lips to hers.

The kiss was gentler than Alice expected. And when it was over, it left her wanting more.

"Is my face blue?" she asked.

"Looks like you have dark lipstick on. Listen, I'm over this party. Did you drive here?"

"No, walked. You?"

"Yeah, me too. Can I walk you home?"

"Let me check with my roommates."

Alice fished her phone out of the small clutch strapped across her torso to text Madison and Haley. Neither texted back.

"I'm afraid my roommates have gone to visit the Smurfs' village," Alice said. "We can go if you want; I just have to grab my jacket, I left it downstairs. You came bare-chested in this cold?"

"Hah, no. I left my hoodie in a room." Peter sprang up and offered her a hand. "I'll go grab it and meet you by the door."

Alice ignored the blue hand and stood up on her own. "Cool. See you downstairs."

Peter let his hand drop and gave her a peck on the lips before hurrying down the corridor.

Alice hopped down the stairs and mercifully found her jacket on its hanger, undamaged. It was always a gamble to leave outerwear unsupervised at house parties; there was a good chance you'd never see it again. As she was pulling on her jacket, Alice caught a flash of white and blue out of the corner of her eye.

She turned around, saying, "You were quick."

But she didn't find the Smurf she was expecting staring back at her. She found Jack.

Six

Jack

"Your face is half blue," Jack said, swiping a thumb from the corner of Alice's mouth down toward her jaw. The blue paint on her lips made him positively murderous.

"And now I imagine you've made it worse," Ice replied defiantly.

"Where are you going?"

"Peter is walking me home."

"Ice, don't." Jack stepped forward but stopped as she backtracked. "I get you're mad at me for what happened today—"

She cut him off. "This has nothing to do with you."

"Don't bullshit me."

"I'm not." Ice stared him down. "Earlier… I was upset about Ethan dumping me. Now I want to blow off steam, and Peter's a charmer. What's your problem?"

Yeah. What was his problem? He'd seen her date before, no problema. He was cool, happy even, with her dating other guys. *But not Peter. Mister NBA was the problem.* Why? Jack wasn't sure, but he knew he didn't want Alice to have anything to do with his captain.

"He's not… What I mean is, I've told you how Peter is with girls. Why would you go home with him?"

"To have fun?" Ice challenged. "Relax! I'm not shopping for a husband."

"Ice, don't be like that."

Alice narrowed her eyes. "Be like what, exactly?"

"This is not you. Come on, I'm taking you home." Jack made to grab her elbow, but she recoiled. He wasn't sure if it was to avoid his touch, the body paint, or both.

"I'm not going anywhere with you. You've made it clear you're only interested in being my friend, and guess what? I don't need a *friend* tonight, I need a *man*."

As if on cue, a hand slapped his shoulder. "My man!" Peter said. "Keeping my lady company? Where did you put your nurse?"

"She had to go to the bathroom," Jack replied, stiffening. All of a sudden, Peter had become the most irritating person he knew, with his swagger and his constant *my man-ing*.

"Might take the lady some time. I just passed the door and there's a line," Peter informed him. "I'm taking off." Peter leaned in and added in a low voice, "And I hope this kitten doesn't have claws. Then again, that could be fun too."

Jack felt an impulse to throttle his friend. Instead, he made an effort to stay calm. "The party's just started and you're going home already?"

"It's not that great of a party," Alice interrupted. "We're going. If you see Madison or Haley, can you tell them I went home? I've texted them, but just in case..."

"Sure." Jack shrugged. Alice pushed past him to get out. Unable to stop her, Jack tugged Peter's arm and whispered in his ear, "Be nice to her. She's a friend."

Peter gave him a foxy smile. "Hey, I'm always nice to the ladies."

Peter made to follow Alice, but Jack held him back. "I'm serious."

"Chill, my man. I'll treat her with white gloves."

Reluctantly, Jack let him go. He cringed as he watched Peter wrap one arm around Alice's shoulders as they headed for the door. She never looked back.

Suddenly, the party seemed incredibly dull. All Jack wanted was to go home and wash off the body paint that had dried hard on his skin and now stretched and pulled with every movement he made. But going home alone wasn't an option. He'd be stuck thinking about Alice and Peter together. Jack shook the image away. He was overreacting. Ice never slept with anyone on a first date, let alone after a trashy party. She might be mad at him, but she wasn't going to sleep with Peter tonight. And Peter didn't like it when girls didn't sleep with him on the first night. He didn't have the patience to wait. The whole thing would blow up before it even started. Jack had nothing to worry about.

Jack marched to the bar, popped a Jell-O shot in his mouth, and then another. He searched the countertop for a clean cup, filled it with ice from the fridge, poured himself an unhealthy amount of vodka, and topped up the cup with a splash of lemon soda.

"There you are," the nurse said. Jack couldn't remember her name. "I thought I'd lost you."

"I was just mixing myself a drink. You want something?"

"What are you having?" She stole the cup from him and grimaced after taking a sip. "Blech, too strong for me." She gave the cup back. "But I'll do a Jell-O shot. You want one?"

"Sure." Jack dropped his too-strong drink on the counter and took the shot, his third in as many minutes.

Ready for the alcohol to kick in, Jack waited for the nurse to put down her glass before he cupped her face to kiss her. As he moved one hand to her back to pull her closer, she grabbed both his hands and kept them away from her body.

"You'll make me blue," she said, pulling away from him.

"You're already blue," he said, looking at her lips and thinking at once of another set of blue-stained lips.

The nurse giggled and wiped her mouth with a napkin. Jack swallowed another shot and gave one to her as well.

"The Smurfs idea is cool, but it can't be comfortable," she said.

"It was a much cooler costume in theory. But this blue paint is getting really itchy."

"We should wash it off," the nurse said suggestively.

"We?"

"Unless you prefer to shower alone."

"I don't." Jack downed another shot and gestured toward the door. "Let's get out of here."

He grabbed his old sweatshirt from under a couple of dudes sitting on the couch and guided the nurse to the front of the house.

Outside, when the cold night air hit his face, Jack paused. He threw a side-glance at the girl walking next to him. What was he doing? He could go home and shower alone, instead of sleeping with the umpteenth girl who meant nothing to him and whose name he couldn't even remember. Maybe it was time to straighten his head, be serious with someone he really cared about. *Ice.*

Jack was about to open his mouth to say he'd changed his mind, when a slow burning started in his stomach and his vision fogged. It was as if all the alcohol in the Jell-O shots suddenly released into his system. Jack staggered sideways and dropped a heavy arm around the nurse's shoulders, all thoughts of redemption forgotten.

Seven

Alice

Now that she was walking home alone with Peter, with Jack out of the picture, Alice didn't feel so bold anymore. What was she doing with a guy she knew nothing about? Was making Jack jealous really worth it? She doubted Peter could give her much more than that. If half the stories Jack had told her about him were true, Jack was practically a monk compared to Peter.

Alice wished she knew what his face looked like without all that blue paint. Not knowing was bothering her more than it should.

"You've gone all quiet on me," Peter said.

"I can't help but think I've no idea what your face looks like."

"We can solve that tomorrow. For now, you can stare at my pretty eyes." He batted his lashes at her.

Alice chuckled. "Is there going to be a tomorrow?"

"I hope so. I've promised to explain how to play basketball, remember?"

"You mean a practical lesson?"

"If you'd like. The coach has left me the keys to the Lavietes Pavilion; it's really cool when it's empty. We could take a couple shots."

"You want me to actually play?"

He stopped and grabbed Alice by the waist, pulling her in front of him. She stiffened, worrying about the paint getting all over her jacket. Then she dismissed the concern; the waterproof fabric wouldn't be hard to wash.

"I'd love to play with you," he said, looking her straight in the eyes. The intensity of his stare dazzled her. "Can we call it a date?"

"Your eyes really are pretty," Alice teased. "So I'm going to say yes."

He leaned in to kiss her. Alice didn't care if this was a mistake; having Peter kiss her was great, and Jack could go to hell for all she cared right now. *This is not you,* he'd told her. But this was exactly her! She was a woman who liked to be kissed by handsome—allegedly—men. She wasn't a nun.

A cold blast of air blew in from behind her, making the hair on her nape stand up and sending a shiver down her spine.

"You're trembling," Peter said, pulling back and massaging her arms with his hands.

"It's cold, and I'm not exactly covered up."

House parties required bringing only the minimum wardrobe. So Alice was standing in the cold of November wearing a flimsy jumpsuit, an older, not-warm-enough jacket, and no gloves, hat, or scarf.

"Yeah, me neither." Peter, with his bare legs, was even more poorly equipped for the chilly air. "Let's get you home."

They walked in silence for another ten minutes until Alice stopped in front of her building. Next to her, Peter kept hopping from one leg to the other. The exposed skin under his shorts sent a shiver down her back.

"This is me," Alice said. "You want to come in? We have a coffeemaker in the hall," she added, to make it clear this wasn't an invitation to her room. "I could make you something hot before you have to walk home."

"Yeah, that'd be great. I'm freezing."

Inside, she made a pot of decaf, which they drank seated at one of the tables. Alice would have preferred the cozy armchairs by the fire, even if it wasn't lit, but she was afraid Peter would stain them. Plastic chairs were easier to wipe clean.

They chatted, enjoying their hot drinks, and Alice soon lost track of the hour. It wasn't until Madison staggered in the front door, barely standing, that Alice realized how much time had passed.

She threw Peter an apologetic look. "I think I'd better go take care of my roommate before she wrecks our apartment."

"Yeah," Peter agreed. "She looks pretty wasted."

Madison was having a silent argument with the elevator. She kept pushing a button that wasn't really a button and started to rage when the little lights signaling the elevator was on call wouldn't light up. Madison increased her efforts, stabbing the plaque with her finger.

"Yep, she does." Alice nodded.

"This dried-up paint is making it painful to talk, anyway," Peter added.

"Is kissing painful too?"

Peter cupped her face with his hands. "I'll take the pain like a man." He kissed her goodnight. "I'll pick you up here tomorrow at two-ish?"

"Sure. I'll leave you my number just in case."

They exchanged contact information, and Peter gave her a quick peck on the lips before jogging out into the night. Alice didn't envy him the walk—or run—home one bit.

Alice joined Madison in front of the elevator. "Here." She pushed the up arrow.

"Was that a Smurf?" Madison asked.

"Yeah."

There was a ding, a swipe of metallic doors, and they stepped inside the elevator.

"I hate Smurfs," Madison said.

"I thought you were with one."

"No, I left for a second to get a drink and, poof, he disappeared with another girl." Madison scoffed. "Story of my life."

Madison had a lot of confidence issues and a huge inferiority complex.

"So, where were you all this time?"

"Haley and I party hopped, and I drank too much."

"You don't say. Where's Haley?"

"She met a guy and left with him."

Alice scoffed. "Another masked dude?"

Haley had been obsessing for months over a guy she'd met at a Venetian Masquerade Ball. After dancing with him most of the night, she'd lost him without ever learning his name, or even what his face looked like.

Madison shrugged. "If that does it for her."

As they reached their floor, Alice helped Madison walk to her room and helped her out of her angel costume. Her friend's beautiful blonde hair was all ruffled and impossibly tangled. It'd be a bitch to comb through the next morning.

"Did our plan work?" Madison asked as Alice tucked her into bed. "Was Jack jealous?"

"I think so." Alice smirked. "The Smurf downstairs was his best friend and favorite wingman. Jack didn't seem happy when I left with him."

"Good for you." Madison patted her on the arm. "Now I have to sleep. I'm really tired…" She closed her eyes and her head lolled to the side of the pillow.

Alice kissed Madison's forehead and retreated to her room. Blue tried to sneak out, but she snatched him up and closed the door.

"Here." She kissed him goodnight and dropped the bunny in his cage, leaving its door open so that if Blue wanted to take a night stroll, he could.

Alice quickly readied for bed, but it took her a while to drift off to sleep. She didn't know what to expect from her date tomorrow. Regardless of what Jack said, Peter hadn't tried anything with her tonight. He couldn't be the bastard Jack had made him out to be. And what about Jack? Had he gone home with Becky? Was he with her right now?

As she tossed in bed, Alice tried to convince herself she didn't care where Jack was or what he was doing. *Or with whom.*

Eight

Jack

Jack woke up staring at a ceiling that wasn't his own. He peeked under the bed sheets—he was naked, and his skin had returned to its normal color. The nurse had done a thorough job of cleaning him last night. She stirred beside him, and Jack sighed.

This was the hard part. The wake-up call could go one of three ways.

One: The girl he'd slept with didn't care that this had been a one night stand with no possible future. (This was the best-case scenario.)

Two: The girl *did* care, but pretended she didn't to either save face or to try to convince him she was cool to date. Still good.

Three: The girl did care and was a crier and/or a screamer. Criers and screamers ranked equally bad on the scale of unpleasant, morning-after talks, beaten only by a combination of the two.

Jack really wasn't in the mood for a shouting match. His head was throbbing, and he needed another hot shower—alone this time. Maybe he could sneak out before she woke up. Pity he was trapped against the wall and not on the easy-escape side of the bed. He could try to climb over the nurse without waking her, but it didn't seem likely.

The nurse stretched. "Morning," she said.

Jack sighed again. Time for *the talk.*

The girl got up immediately without trying to cuddle—a promising sign. She got dressed, and Jack did the same, taking in the whole room as he searched for the exit door.

"Stop acting like a trapped animal," said the nurse, who was no longer dressed as a nurse—she was wearing a pair of black leggings and a Harvard sweatshirt. "I'm not going to make a scene if that's what you're worried about. I'll make you a cup of coffee—if you want it—and send you on your way. No drama."

Jack was surprised. He thought he'd seen it all, but this was a new level of unconcernedness. "I'll take the coffee," he said.

"Milk, sugar, black?"

"Black is cool."

The studio apartment was tiny. The bed doubled as a couch, and the kitchenette was stuffed in a small corner with barely a bar and two stools. Jack sat on one.

The nurse placed a steamy mug on the countertop. "Here's your coffee."

"Thanks, mmm…"

"Becky. The name's Becky."

"I knew," Jack lied.

She raised an eyebrow. "No need to pretend here."

Jack couldn't help asking, "So, we're cool?" He usually avoided these questions like the plague.

"Yeah."

"How come?" And here he was asking one after the other.

"I'm too busy with school to have or want a boyfriend. Alice told me you'd be perfect for a night of fun, so this"—

she flipped a finger between them—"is it. Plain and simple. No strings attached."

Jack grimaced. "Great!"

This should've been Jack's dream morning-after speech, but somehow it depressed him. He felt *used.* Jack slapped his face with his hands to get a grip on himself; he was turning into a girl. What bothered him the most was that Alice had told this girl—Becky—he was one-night-stand material. It hurt, even if it was true. And why had Alice pushed Becky into his arms? After her stunt at the library, it made little sense.

Yesterday afternoon she'd tried to kiss him, and he suspected there were feelings involved. He was sure it wasn't by chance she'd somehow showed up at the same Halloween party just a few hours later. Had she wanted to make him jealous? He would have assumed that was the case, except the whole night she'd acted as if nothing had happened between them. She'd barely spoken to him, pushed him to hook up with another girl, and then she'd left with Peter.

Jack's blood boiled. If this was all a perverse plan to make him jealous, it was working. The thought of Alice and Peter together made his seat too hot. He'd never been jealous of Alice's boyfriends, but for some inexplicable reason, Peter was different. Jack had to know what had happened, or, hopefully, what hadn't happened between them last night.

He finished the coffee and stood. "Well, Becky, thanks so much for the coffee"—Jack stroked the back of his head with one hand, embarrassed—"and everything else. I'll get out of here." Jack peeked out the window; he had no idea where Becky lived, or how they'd gotten here last night. "Err… Where's 'here?'"

"We're on Litchfield street. It's a quick walk to campus."

"I'm making it a morning run." He was still wearing his sporty shorts and an old sweatshirt. Mornings in Cambridge in November were viciously cold.

Becky stared, unimpressed. "Even quicker."

She walked him to the door and opened it for him; she was kicking him out. It was a weird novelty for Jack.

"Do we hug goodbye?" he asked.

"Sure." She gave him an unconcerned hug and waved him goodbye.

Jack jogged home. He beat his roommate to the bathroom and took a long, hot shower followed by a huge, alcohol-draining breakfast. By the time he was done, it was already mid-morning. It was time to make a call. He scrolled through his contacts with his thumb and tapped on Peter's name.

Peter picked up on the second ring. "Sullivan, my man, what's up?"

"Hey, Captain, you up for a one-on-one game later?"

"Can't do," Peter answered, and alarm bells went off inside Jack's head. "I have a date," he added, confirming his fears.

Jack oh-so-casually asked, "Someone I know?"

"Yep, that girl from your concentration, Alice Brown. I'm giving her a behind-the-scenes of the Lavietes."

Jack ground his teeth and tried to speak in a normal voice. "You guys hit it off, then?"

"Nah." Relief washed over Jack as Peter continued, "Turns out the blue paint was great to attract the attention, but a big turn off for the ladies. How did it go with your nurse?"

"I had her bathe me first," Jack replied smugly.

"Ooooh, my man!" Peter hollered. "I should take that page out of your book. You're a genius."

"So you went to bed early? It wasn't even midnight when you left."

"No, the kitten kept me up talking until her roommate came home wasted."

Jack stared at the phone, not sure he'd heard right. "You were up all night *talking?*"

"Yeah. Your friend was cool, and the paint was too weird anyway. We'll see how it goes today."

Jack was tense again. "What, do you plan to have sex on the court?" he snapped. "If the coach catches you, you're dead."

"Not on the court." Peter chuckled. "Maybe later. Anyway, your Alice seems more of a slow burner."

Exactly, *his* Alice. "And you're okay with waiting?"

"I kind of like this girl."

Why, of all girls, did Peter have to walk the line for Ice? "That's a first."

"Who knows, my man; maybe she'll take one look at my face and decide I'm gross." Jack doubted it. "She kept saying she was bothered she couldn't picture how I looked under all the paint."

"I'd run for the hills if I saw your ugly face," Jack joked.

Peter laughed. "All right, buddy, I've gotta run too. See you tomorrow at practice, yeah?"

"Yeah, I'll talk to you later."

"Later."

Peter hung up.

Jack stood up and hurled his phone at the bed. It bounced off and landed on the carpet unscathed. Jack kicked it under the bed. What the hell was happening to him? Peter was behaving, and it made him angry instead of relieved. Why was he so mad? *Who* was he mad at? Alice? Peter? Himself?

On impulse, Jack picked up his gym duffel bag and decided to go to the MAC and work off some steam. Staying home and brooding definitely wasn't an option. Instead, he'd do some cardio to sweat out the hangover, and maybe also some weight training. Homework would keep him busy for the rest of the afternoon. Jack couldn't afford to fall behind, not with the basketball season kicking off next weekend.

An evil grin spread on his lips as Jack studied the practice schedule hanging over his bed. He wouldn't have much idle time in the coming months, but neither would Peter have much time to woo Alice. *Aha!*

Nine

Alice

Madison staggered into Alice's room, dragging her feet behind her, and sat on the empty bed. "I'm never going to drink again."

Alice stopped leafing through her closet to look at her friend. "That's what every college kid says after a great Halloween party."

"Meh, the party kind of sucked."

"Agreed." Alice nodded. "At least it got me a date."

"About that. What's your plan here?"

"Actually, I don't have one." Alice resumed her shuffling of clothes. "Thinking I could make Jack jealous was stupid."

"I thought it worked."

"Yeah, me too, until I read this." Alice abandoned her closet again, took her phone out of her jeans' pocket, and handed it to Madison. "It's the first message on WhatsApp."

Becky had sent her a too-graphic text about her showering activities with Jack.

"Ew," was Madison's sole comment.

"I know," Alice sighed. "Jack definitely wasn't heartbroken about me going home with Peter."

"So you're dating his friend now? Doesn't he have the worst reputation?"

"He does, but so far he's been nice."

"You like him?"

"Too early to say." Alice shrugged. "Let me see his face first, without all that blue paint."

Madison tapped the phone. "Want me to find the Crimson roster pics on their website?"

"Actually, I prefer it to be a surprise."

"And if he's ugly?"

"I don't think he is." Alice smiled a secret smile. "Anyway, a face alone doesn't do it for me. I need to feel a connection, a spark."

"But isn't he your typical athlete jerk?" Madison insisted.

"Can't say yet." Alice closed the room door before Blue could make a run for it. "I agree with you. On paper, his CV is bad, but last night felt so easy talking to him. It felt right."

"You're giving up on Jack then?"

Alice wasn't sure; the text from Becky had churned her stomach. Her feelings toward Jack right now were more violent than loving.

"I don't know," she admitted. "Jack isn't stupid. He knows yesterday wasn't just about a rebound, no matter what I said afterward. If he wants to make something out of it, he knows where to find me. In the meantime, I'll live my life."

Madison captured a sulky-looking Blue as he hopped near the bed. "With his best friend?" she asked, stroking the bunny.

"Well, I'm not going to stay single and wait for Jack to make up his mind."

"But if you go out with Peter, doesn't that make you off-limits for Jack, even if he's into you?"

"Why?"

"I don't know." Madison shrugged. "Don't they have a bro code—'Bros before Hoes,' or something like that?"

"Huh. I hadn't thought about that." Was she making a mistake? No, Alice couldn't second-guess herself like this. "If they have a secret code, I know nothing about it," she told Madison. "Anyway, it's nothing serious with Peter. He's just a much-needed distraction."

"If you say so." Madison sounded unconvinced. "Have you decided what to wear?"

Alice turned back toward her closet. "No. I've never been on a sporty date before."

"You can borrow my new PINK set if you want."

"You're a lifesaver!" Alice jumped on her bed to hug Madison. Blue squealed in protest.

***

At two p.m., Peter texted Alice he was on his way. She took the elevator to the lobby and waited for him behind the hall's glass doors, avoiding the outside cold.

When a tall guy jogged up the steps, she didn't recognize Peter, not until he waved and smiled from behind the glass. Alice's breath caught in her throat. Peter was a Jake Gyllenhaal lookalike, much better looking than she expected. She reminded herself that looks meant nothing and put her woolen gloves on before opening the door.

"Hey, you," she said, feeling shy.

He gave her a quick hug and flashed her a grin. "So, did I pass the face test?"

Alice beamed back. "You know you did."

He winked. "Shall we go?"

They entered Lavietes Pavilion from a secondary

access, and Peter led the way to the basketball court. He took off his jacket and beanie. Alice watched him, thinking she'd never seen a guy look that sexy in sportswear. She followed his lead and peeled off her coat, hat, scarf, and gloves, setting them on another plastic chair.

Alice sized up the stadium; it was much bigger than she had expected. Weird that they allowed players to come in when it was closed.

"Are you sure we're allowed in here?" Alice asked.

"Not really."

Alice glared at Peter. "What do you mean?"

"The coach didn't exactly give me the keys; I might've lifted them from him."

"Are you crazy?" Her mouth gaped open before she started to panic. "We could get expelled! You could get kicked off the team…"

"Nah," Peter said, unfazed. "I'm too good a player to kick me off. Relax; no one's coming today. Coach Morrison gave us a free day. Last one of the season, probably."

Alice still wasn't convinced about staying. "How come?"

"We have our first game next Saturday, so no free weekends until March. The coach told us to have fun on Halloween night, rest today, and get ready to sweat on Monday."

Alice let his enthusiasm infect her, and she relaxed. "Did he also tell you to get blue?"

"No, that was the team's personal initiative."

Alice stared around the court. "So this is where the magic happens?"

"Yep. Wait here."

Peter unlocked another door—probably a storeroom—disappeared inside, and came back bouncing an orange ball. He stopped close to her and made the ball spin on his index finger.

"Are you trying to impress me?"

"Are you impressed?"

"Not yet."

"How about now?" Peter turned toward the right basket, bent his knees, and made the shot from half a court away.

Holding her breath, Alice watched the ball fly across the room. It went right through the metal hoop, barely making the net move. Peter was already running after it.

"You're such a showoff," she said after he came back to stand beside her. "So, how does this game work?"

Peter bounced the ball again while he explained. "Varsity rules are different from the real thing." Every two or three bounces, he made the ball loop between his legs in a move Alice was sure was not as easy as it looked. "Each team has five players on the court, and there's one captain."

Alice smiled. "Let me guess—that's you?"

"You guessed right."

He continued with his Basketball 101, and Alice listened patiently. Peter was so passionate he could convert even an anti-sports girl like her.

When Alice's head started to spin with all the rules, Peter finally said, "That's the basics—oh, also, you have to dribble the ball at all times. You can't run across the court holding it. More than three steps"—he stopped the ball and made three demonstrative steps—"and you lose the play. You want to try a shot?"

Alice suddenly felt self-conscious. "You'll have to show me how; my last attempt was in fifth grade or something."

"Come here."

Alice joined Peter at the free-throw line, and he positioned himself close behind her. A shiver spider-walked down her spine. *What have I gotten myself into?*

"Your right foot should be slightly in front," Peter said, his warm breath trickling down her neck. As he helped her get into the right position, all Alice could focus on was how the front of his leg pressed on the back of hers as he pushed it forward.

"Keep your weight on the balls of your feet," Peter instructed. "And hold the ball like this." He was a good foot taller than Alice, and he showed her how to palm the ball by holding it above her head from behind. The demonstration required him to push his chest against her back, making her skin tingle at the touch. "Here, take it."

Alice took the ball from him and he adjusted her hands on it.

"Now bend your knees and push your hips backward." He pulled gently at her waist, bringing their bodies even closer together, and Alice got body-wide goose bumps.

He let go and circled her. "Elbow up." Peter pushed her ball-supporting arm up about two inches.

"You're bossy," Alice said, straightening.

He chuckled. "Knees bent."

Alice crouched again.

"Now do a little jump and shoot."

Alice gathered momentum in her knees and then straightened her body in a fluid motion, releasing the ball as her feet left the ground. The orange sphere soared up in the air and started its descent toward the rim. For one glorious moment, Alice thought it would go in. Then it bounced off the hoop and fell out of the net.

"Almost," she said.

"Not bad for a first try." Peter ran after the ball. "Here, try again." He threw the ball at her.

She caught it and got back into position.

After fifteen minutes of free shooting, Alice's arms began to hurt. She'd never realized how heavy the ball could become. "I'm tired. Can we take a break?"

"Wait here." Peter disappeared again and came back with a blue throw mat. He sat on it and patted the empty space next to him.

Alice joined him. "Have you always wanted to play basketball?"

"Not exactly, but when I turned fourteen I shot up a foot, and I think my height decided for me."

"How tall are you?" Alice studied him, trying to gauge his height in her head. "Six five?"

"Six seven."

"Whoa."

Peter hooked an arm around her waist and pulled her closer. "You don't play any sports, then?"

"I used to do gymnastics," Alice said. "But it was never professional or anything."

"You mean you used to do all those scary jumps and weird contortions?"

"They're not so scary once you get the hang of them."

"Still badass. Want to show me?"

She smiled. "I'm way out of practice. But I can show you a video of when I was eleven."

"I'd love to see it. Did you have one of those sparkly costumes on?"

Alice blushed and changed the subject; she didn't want

Peter picturing her in a stupid costume. "How come you're spending your last free afternoon for the next five months with me?"

"There are worse people, no?"

"Thank you very much." She made to swat his shoulder playfully, but he caught her wrist and held it, pulling her toward him.

Alice became suddenly shy under his blue gaze. Even more so when he lifted her chin with his free hand, brushed one thumb across her cheek, and kissed her. They lay back on the mat, still kissing, him on top of her.

The loud sound of a door shutting in the distance interrupted their heated kiss.

"Shit, someone's here." Peter leapt to his feet, and so did Alice.

Peter moved faster than a leopard. He picked up the mat and ran to turn off the light. Alice collected their coats and followed Peter inside a storeroom filled with various training equipment. Peter put the mat back in place, then closed the little room's door. They were left standing in complete darkness.

Peter pressed a finger on her closed lips. "We have to keep quiet," he whispered. "Whatever happens."

"What do you mean?" she hissed, starting to panic.

He brushed his lips against her ear. "Only that if I tickle you, you can't scream." He moved his fingers to her sides and Alice suppressed a giggle, pressing her mouth to his chest. "Quiet," he ordered.

They heard muffled voices coming from the main court, and Peter stopped tickling her. It was scary and exciting, especially when Peter pushed Alice against the vertical pile of mats and left a trail of kisses down her neck. Alice pulled herself up to kiss him on the mouth, completely forgetting the people outside.

She wasn't sure how long they stayed locked in the cramped storeroom, wrapped around each other. But she suspected their kisses lasted well beyond the moment the voices outside went gone quiet.

"I think it's safe to go out," Peter whispered in her ear. "But let me check first."

He moved away from her and used his phone as a torch to find the handle. He pulled the door open, letting in a sliver of faint light.

"I think we're good," Peter said, opening the door completely. "But we'd better go."

They hastily threw on their coats and snuck out of the pavilion by the same door they'd used to get in. Outside, it was already dark. Alice checked her watch; time with Peter had flown by again. They grabbed a quick bite to eat, and then Peter walked her back to her building.

Alice stepped up onto the first step leading to the entrance door. "This way I'm only half a foot shorter than you," she said, placing her hands on his shoulders. Peter wrapped his arms around her waist.

"Have I earned a next date?" he asked.

"You get points for the basketball lesson, but lose some for almost getting us caught." She paused. "However, you do get bonuses for your kissing-in-the-dark skills."

No more encouragement was needed for him to demonstrate those skills again.

"Was that a yes?" he asked after the kiss.

"Yeah." Alice nodded. "What should we do next? Break into the library at night?"

"How about something homier?"

"Like what?"

"Dinner, prepared by yours truly?"

Alice was surprised. "You can cook?"

Peter winked. "One of my other secret skills."

"I'd love to." Alice smiled. "When?"

"Ah." Peter scratched his head. "Between classes and practice, I'm conscripted until next Sunday. Early dinner?"

"It's a date." Alice smashed an imaginary gavel on an imaginary bench. "Sunday sounds great, and I have a busy week too."

Peter's eyes sparkled with another idea. "Hey," he said. "We play McGill Saturday night—why don't you come to watch the game?"

Alice really hated sports, but how could she say no? "Okay. Do I have to get tickets?"

"This one's free admission," Peter said. "Just arrive early to get decent seats."

"Will do," Alice said. He was cooking her dinner; she could endure *one* game. And she would force Haley and Madison to go with her so she wouldn't be alone and bored the whole time.

"I'm counting on it," he said.

Alice gave him another kiss. Then she hopped up the steps and hurried inside her building, feeling giddier than she deemed wise.

Ten

Jack

Jack was ten minutes late for his nine a.m. Organic Chemistry class, despite the fact that he'd changed at top speed after practice and ran here straight from the gym. Luckily, the professor had his back turned to the class as he wrote today's lesson plan on the board, allowing Jack to sneak in undetected.

As he jogged down the stairs of the classroom, Jack's muscles ached and his mood was at an all-time low. Coach Morrison wanted to kick off the season with a victory against McGill, resulting in a particularly nasty workout. But it was the short chat with Peter beforehand that left Jack the sorest. As they changed in the locker room, the captain had given him the highlights of his date with Ice the day before. Jack had barely heard anything the coach said all practice, too busy imagining Alice and Peter locked together in that dark storeroom.

He paused halfway down the stairs and searched for the back of Alice's head in the crowded lecture hall. It took him a minute to recognize her as the brunette sitting in their usual spot two rows from the front. The color change was doing weird things to him. He'd never thought he preferred brunettes over blondes or redheads. Yet for Ice, Jack was sure he preferred her as a brunette. He hopped down the steps and took his spot next to her.

"What did I miss?" he asked.

"Not much." Ice didn't turn to look at him, nor did she

stop taking notes. "We're just getting started on multi-step organic synthesis. Did you have breakfast?"

"No," Jack whispered. "The coach kept us until the last minute."

Ice abandoned her notepad to reach into her bag and take out an energy bar. This was why she was his best friend. She always carried around a supply of energy bars for him, exactly for days like this. Okay, so Ice was acting normal, showing no hard feelings over Saturday. But Jack couldn't relax—even if he'd dodged an uncomfortable conversation about the library, Ice's date with Peter was still bugging him.

"Here." She also handed him a silver thermos. "There's some coffee left. It shouldn't be cold yet."

"You're a life saver."

Technically speaking, food and drinks weren't allowed in class, but the rule was widely overlooked around campus. Especially where coffee was concerned.

Jack finished his breakfast and tried to follow the lecture. Ice was pretending nothing had happened, and Jack wanted to pretend, too. He wanted to keep his mouth shut but found he couldn't. "Did you have fun yesterday?" he asked.

Alice finally turned toward him with a sharp look. Yeah, dark hair definitely suited her best; it brought out her eyes. She studied his face for a few seconds before speaking. "If you're asking, I guess you already know."

True. They hadn't spoken after the party, and she hadn't told him she was going on a date with Peter. She must've guessed Peter had told him.

"Yeah, Peter mentioned your date this morning."

Professor Procter raised his voice pointedly.

Alice scribbled something on her notepad and edged it toward Jack.

Talk later. Deal?

As he read, she underlined the writing twice. A final statement.

Jack mouthed, "Deal," and took out his Organic Chemistry book, determined to finally concentrate on the lesson. He could talk to her between classes.

He had to wait until their lunch break to broach the Peter subject again. They had a morning full of lectures, and after each one ended, Alice was out of her seat, down the stairs, and by the door in seconds. She'd done her best to avoid talking to him. But as they walked toward the cafeteria, she had no escape.

"So," he started, "you moved on pretty quickly from Ethan."

"Not as quick as you, apparently."

"Meaning?"

Alice gave him that seething look again. "Did you have fun taking off all that blue paint?"

Touché. She knew about the nurse. Becky had to have a flaw, right? She wasn't a morning-after drama queen, but she had a big mouth.

"I never said I was in love with Lori," Jack said, trying to justify his actions.

"Neither was I with Ethan," Ice countered.

"Okay, but you were serious about him."

"My bad."

Jack let out an exasperated, "Come on, Ice."

"What?" She played dumb.

"You're always serious when you date."

"So?"

"So you shouldn't date guys like Peter—or myself, for that matter."

Ice stopped walking. "Why do you have a problem with him?"

"He's not good when it comes to girls, trust me on this."

"He's been perfectly nice to me."

"It's only been two days."

"Well, you'd better get used to it." Alice positively glowered at him. "I'm coming to the game Saturday, and we have another date Sunday."

"What?" Jack asked, shocked. "You've never come to a game before."

"You never asked."

"Because I know you hate sports."

"I don't hate sports," Alice said. "I don't particularly enjoy them, but it doesn't mean I can't watch a game. It was fun playing yesterday."

"You had fun playing basketball, or you had fun in the storeroom?" Jack inwardly cringed at how petty he sounded.

"Both, if you really have to know," she hissed.

"You're making a mistake."

"Listen, Jack." Alice rolled her eyes. "Your objections have been duly noted. But right now I like Peter, he makes me feel good, and I want to feel good. I need to. So I'll keep dating him. If or when he does something I don't like, I'll stop. End of story."

"Are you going to sleep with him?"

"What if I am?"

"He'll just use you."

"Why?" She pursed her lips. "You think it's impossible for a guy to want to date me for more than a few months?"

"A few months?" Jack laughed. "With Peter, you'll be lucky if it turns into a few weeks before he moves on to someone else. If he's not already seeing some other girl on the side. It wouldn't be the first time."

"And why can't he be different for me?"

"Guys like him just aren't."

"You mean guys like *you!*" Alice splayed her arms to her sides. "You're such a hypocrite."

"Why?"

"You sleep your way around campus and now you're bashing Peter for his low moral standards?"

"I'm just warning you." Jack wanted to grab her by the shoulders and shake some sense into her. "If you want to make a fool of yourself, be my guest."

"You know what? Go to hell." Alice's eyes became watery and her lower lip trembled as she repeated, "You just go to hell."

She stormed away, not looking back, and Jack was too mad to run after her. He walked in the opposite direction, heading to a different café.

What was happening to him? Alice was right. He was in no position to judge Peter; their attitude toward girls was the same. Ice should steer clear of them both. Imagining her in bed with Peter made Jack see red. If Alice wasn't going to listen to him, he'd have to distract Peter from her. Yeah, find a hot girl for his friend and have him forget Ice for good. It was all in her best interest. He'd be doing her a favor.

Eleven
Alice

After their argument on Monday, Alice tried to give Jack the haughty silent treatment. It didn't work; Jack didn't let her go a day not talking to him. At their next shared lesson, he switched on the charm and soon he had her bent in two laughing her head off. After softening her up, he apologized and said he shouldn't be meddling in her love life. Jack explained he had seen many girls hurt by Peter, and that he was simply worried about her. But he understood she was a big girl and that she could make her own decisions. He was just a concerned friend.

Just. A. Friend. Words Alice officially hated.

How could three simple words send her emotions spiraling?

Alice had to get him out of her head. She'd been obsessing about Jack since freshman year; it was about time she accepted they weren't going to happen as a couple. He'd made it perfectly clear he wasn't interested. All that crap about not wanting to ruin their friendship was just that: crap. If a guy, especially one with Jack's sex drive, was interested, it was impossible to be that rational. To have the amount of self-control he'd shown her when she offered herself up on a silver platter. He simply didn't like her, not in the way she wanted him to. She should've known from that first humiliating time he'd made it stark clear he'd never look at her any other way.

***

Alice had spent the entire Saturday afternoon choosing an outfit that would send the message: you want to spend the rest of your life with me, but I'm not trying too hard. It was a difficult one to pull off, especially if she added the keep-me-warm-in-winter requirement. It the end, she'd opted for a homey-sexy look as opposed to outright-sexy: uber-tight jeans, ankle boots, and a cream sweater that hugged her curves in all the right places.

She still couldn't believe Jack had finally asked her to go on a real date with him. "Dinner tomorrow night, deal?" he'd asked her the day before at the end of class. It hadn't been a declaration of undying love, but it was an improvement from meeting up for coffee or going to the library to study. Dinner on a Saturday night meant serious business.

Alice entered the restaurant with a pounding heart and flushed cheeks—reddened not just by the sudden warmth of the place, but by who was waiting for her inside. She spotted Jack sitting in a high-backed booth, half hidden by the booth in front of him. From the entrance, Alice could only see his right side. He was reading a menu.

As if he felt her looking at him, he lifted his gaze and they locked eyes. Alice's world tilted. Hers wasn't a simple crush; she had fallen head-over-heels for Jack. He got up, flashing a wild grin, and walked toward her. As he hugged her hello, Alice inhaled his scent—a mix of his shaving gel and his natural odor—and her stomach exploded with butterflies.

"You came alone?" Jack asked.

He seemed surprised.

"Yeah?"

She followed Jack back to the booth only to see a pretty girl already occupying the seat closest to the wall.

"Ice, this is Olivia." Jack made the introductions. "Olivia, meet Alice."

Olivia*?* HAS HE ASKED ME OUT TO INTRODUCE ME TO HIS GIRLFRIEND*? Alice screamed inside her head. No! This wasn't happening. This couldn't happen.*

It could, and it was.

Alice watched the girl get up as if in slow motion. Her bubble of happiness had transformed in a water bubble that slowed everything down and made voices sound deep and distorted.

In her slow motion voice, Olivia said, "Noooice tooo meeeet yoooouuu." She extended a manicured hand.

Muscle-memory made Alice stretch out her arm and take Olivia's hand. Her lips froze in a polite expression—one she hoped didn't look too strained—as she willed herself to sit opposite the happy couple. She prayed she wouldn't start crying in front of them, although angry tears were already welling in her eyes.

Alice dabbed at the corner of her eyes with the sleeve of her sweater. "Gosh, it was windy outside," she said to explain the gesture.

"We were thinking of catching a movie later," Jack said.

At least this torture session would be short-lived. Alice calculated how long her agony would last. It was a few minutes past seven. Surely, they'd want to catch the eight-thirty show, nine at the latest. The walk to the movie theater took fifteen minutes, plus ten to get the tickets... They had to leave in an hour, an hour and a half tops. She could survive sixty minutes of this. She didn't have another choice.

"Do you have any plans for later?" Jack asked.

Alice's plan had been to spend the night in Jack's arms making love to him for the first time.

"Plans?" You mean besides crying myself to death? *"I have a... um... sorority meeting."*

"They make you meet on a Saturday?" Olivia—the nosy bitch—asked.

"It isn't an official meeting, just first year pledges getting together and hanging out."

"It must be nice to be part of a group." Olivia's over polite smile seemed to imply, "See? This is my little group here: Jack and me."

Olivia had possessively linked her arm with Jack's; she was so irritating, Alice felt a swell of anger, envy, and, possibly even, a tiny surge of hatred. She had a mental vision of grabbing the ketchup and mustard bottles—one with each hand—and squeezing them in Olivia's face until they were both empty. As unrealizable as the fantasy was, it gave Alice the strength to endure the next hour.

***

Olivia, like many others after her, had been but a short footnote in Jack's life. Instead, Jack's newfound attitude of acting as if Peter didn't exist stuck around a lot longer. Alice didn't know what to make of this new approach, but she preferred it to the insistent nagging that had preceded it. Jack constantly telling her how a guy like Peter could never fall for her, to Alice translated as Jack telling her how *he* would never fall for her.

Dating someone else had always been the best way to avoid thinking about Jack not liking her, or Jack's new girl-of-the-moment. Maybe Peter wasn't the wisest distraction of choice, but he was good-looking, charming, and so far he'd treated her with nothing but respect. True, he had a reputation. So what? Alice was just looking for a fun pastime to avoid brooding over Jack. She wasn't going to get hurt; she could handle Peter. And if he dumped her, she'd deal with it. Just as she'd dealt with Ethan breaking up with her. Or, more to the point, telling her she'd never been his girlfriend in the first place and that he didn't want to have casual, meaningless sex with her anymore. *Good times…*

Besides, Peter's flirty texts were the only highlight in her otherwise bleak routine. She'd started to look forward to the little red circle with a white number appearing over her WhatsApp icon. They hadn't managed to meet again after their date on Sunday, as both their schedules were packed: classes, his practices, her sorority commitments. Their few free moments did not overlap, but they chatted a lot through texts, and by the time Saturday rolled around, Alice couldn't wait for their dinner the next day. Peter had promised to cook for her, and she was fascinated. Not many college kids had kitchen skills beyond microwaving premade meals.

"Well," Madison said as they entered Lavietes Pavilion with half an hour to spare before the game. "Harvard certainly doesn't push the bling side of varsity sports"

"Why?" Alice asked.

Alice, Madison, and Haley took three seats close to the front. Peter had told her to come early, but they needn't have worried. The stands were still half-empty.

"I watched a game at Notre Dame once, and it was like going to an NBA game," Madison explained. "They had mega screens hanging from the ceiling, videos, music, cheerleaders… Their pavilion is like a real indoor stadium; this looks like a sorry high school gym."

"I thought people only ever went to Notre Dame to watch football," Haley said.

"Football season was over when I visited."

"Why were you in Indiana, anyway?" Alice asked.

"My cousin from my mother's side goes to school there. She's not a Smithson, so she wasn't destined to Harvard-then-Harvard-Law from birth."

Madison's family ran one of the top law firms in Boston. All Smithson kids were expected to graduate from Harvard Law School. Ethan was an alumnus, Georgiana was attending it now, and Madison would apply next year. Alice remembered how Ethan always complained about the suffocating expectations of his family.

"Is the Harvard team any good at basketball?" Alice asked.

Madison shook her head. "I have no idea."

"Neither do I," Haley said. "Anyway, we're here for the tall, pretty boys, so who cares."

"Speaking of, which tall, pretty boy are we concentrating our attention on today?" Madison asked.

"Peter, I think," Alice said.

"So no Jack?" Madison insisted. "Are you suddenly over him?"

"No, I'm not." Alice puffed her cheeks in exasperation. "But he made it clear I'm not his cup of tea. I thought that if—when—I told him how I felt about him, we'd have one of those Hollywood moments a la *When Harry Met Sally*. Unfortunately, I got more of a *He's Just Not That Into You*."

"But you didn't really tell him how you feel," Haley pointed out.

"Thank goodness for that!" Alice cringed at the thought. "At least it wasn't a complete humiliation."

Madison pouted. "Are you sure an 'I'm madly in love with you' speech wouldn't have made a difference?"

"No difference, I'm sure."

"What about Peter?" Haley asked. "You like him?"

"Yeah. He's fun, charming, and he has pretty eyes."

"Isn't he a bit of a… mmm…" Haley let her words hang.

"Man-slut?" Alice supplied. No point in denying it. "Yeah, I think so. But I'm not looking for a serious relationship right now."

"As long as you don't get hurt," Madison said.

"I don't care about him enough to get hurt."

A speaker announcing the two teams silenced Madison's upcoming retort. They stopped talking about the boys and concentrated on ogling them.

"I know number 23." Madison pointed at one of the players. "He's in most of my English classes."

Something in her friend's tone of voice made Alice think Madison had a little crush on the guy.

Haley didn't pick up the vibe. "He's super cute," she said. "What's his name?"

"Scott," Madison said sulkily.

Haley checked the Crimson website on her phone. "Number 23, Scott Williams. He's a junior."

"I told you he's in my class."

"Is he single?" Haley asked.

"Why do you want to know?"

"Relax!" Haley said. "What are you so touchy about?"

It was clear to Alice that Madison was getting territorial, but sometimes Haley could be completely blind to other people's feelings.

"Look." Haley pointed at the court. "He's going for a shot." They all followed the ball as Scott let it go and it flew over the court. "Goal!" Haley shouted, lifting her arms over her head.

"This isn't soccer," Madison snapped.

Haley poked her tongue at Madison and turned to Alice. "You should ask Peter to introduce us."

"Sure," Alice said, taking a mental note to never ever do so.

Madison scoffed, but Haley wasn't looking at her and didn't seem to hear. Then the referee blew the start whistle, and the three of them stopped talking and concentrated on the game.

Alice was no expert, but once the game was over, two facts were clear.

One: Peter was the team's star.

And two: Jack had played like crap.

She looked at him now. Even if Harvard had won to McGill 66 to 63, it was clear Jack had a black temper. As if he felt her staring, he turned toward her. They locked eyes, and his frown deepened. Jack quickly looked away and disappeared into the locker room. Ah, hell, if he wanted to be a sour puss for having played one bad game… This was why she didn't like sports much. Alice hated how a won or lost game—or badly played, in this case—could sway the mood of a person, or an entire city, or even a country. It was so stupid.

She caught Peter's eye next. He shot her a grin; his mood couldn't have been more different from Jack's. Peter blew her a kiss and twirled his index finger in a "later" gesture that she knew meant tomorrow. He had been clear that game nights were reserved for the team. She gave him the thumbs-up and blew a kiss back. Peter waved and then focused his attention on an approaching reporter.

Twelve

Jack

Jack entered the locker room and flung his neck towel down onto a bench. He hurried in and out of the shower before any of his teammates were finished. When Peter eventually jogged into the locker room, Jack was already getting dressed.

The captain did his usual round of high fives and cheered with the rest of the team, then stopped next to Jack. "Sullivan, my man," he said, giving Jack a pat on the shoulder. "It'll go better next time, and we won anyway."

Jack gave him a stiff nod, avoiding catching his eye. He was scared he might punch his friend otherwise. Peter's words of condescension continued to ring in his ears, their implied meaning obvious. Did Peter expect Jack to thank him for saving the game? Fat chance of that. He'd never been jealous of Peter being the better player. Jack cared more about his academic achievements as far as his time at Harvard was concerned. Yet tonight, he was bitterly jealous of Peter's raw talent. He was getting increasingly mad, and it was all Alice's fault.

Jack finished getting dressed, packed his bag, and sat on a bench near his locker to wait for the others to catch up with him. When they were all showered and mostly dressed, Coach Morrison came in for his usual after-game speech. Jack's shoulders slumped, and he prepared himself for another humiliating fifteen minutes.

As expected, praises for Peter were equaled only by

admonishments toward Jack. Harsh, but—thanks to the final victory—brief. Peter had cut his rebuff short by winning the game almost single-handedly; it should have made Jack appreciate his captain. It only made him angrier.

After dinner, a few players decided to go for a nightcap somewhere nearby. Jack was tempted to say goodnight and go sulk in the privacy of his room, but then he noticed Peter join the group. A mean idea struck him. If Peter was going, so would Jack. All it took to end Peter's so-called relationship with Ice was for the captain to go home with a pretty girl. Piece of cake! Peter always ended up sleeping with someone after a victory on the court.

They headed for a cheap beer in The Cambridge Queen's Head, a low-key pub on campus. There were six of them in total, the best regular players. Scott and David Williams, two brothers on the team, went to order for everyone while the others secured a table. Jack was puzzled. It was rare for the two brothers to hang out together; they usually avoided each other. Besides blood ties, the two seemed to have little in common. Scott was warm and easygoing, David cold and detached. Jack was pretty sure they hated each other. He shook the thought away; the Williams brothers weren't his focus right now.

Jack concentrated on the crowd in the pub. Being Saturday night, it was busy and packed with pretty girls. In fact, just as Scott and David returned with their beers, two blonde girls strolled by. One had her hair tied up in a high ponytail; she had a cute smile and big eyes. Pretty. Yet her friend was more attractive with her long, straight hair and doll face.

"Did you guys all swallow a bottle of Skele-Gro as kids?" Ponytail asked, while her friend smiled with a flirtatious twinkle in her eyes.

Jack would've usually focused all his attention on the prettiest girl, but tonight he had a different agenda. He chatted up the ponytailed friend, completely ignoring Doll Face. Out of the corner of his eye, he saw Doll Face's temporary confusion at being overlooked. Then the girl shrugged and turned to talk to the other tall guy standing next to her: Peter.

Jack was only half-following his conversation with Ponytail. He was too busy trying to overhear snippets of what Peter was saying to Doll Face. She was exactly his type, much more than Alice was, especially with her new look.

"Are you even listening to me?" Ponytail asked.

"Yeah, sure," Jack lied.

"So what do you think?"

"About what?"

"Forget it. I'm getting another drink." She left.

Doll Face was still talking to Peter when she noticed her friend was gone.

"I'd better check on my friend," she told Peter. Her tone suggested she didn't actually want to. Jack read her imaginary subtitles: "I want you to tell me to ignore my friend and ask me to stay here."

Jack waited for Peter to use one of his usual get-lucky lines. If he left with this girl, his relationship with Ice would end before it even started.

Instead, Peter just shrugged. "Sure," he said, lifting his glass to drain the last inch of his beer. "I'm heading home anyway."

Hit by her second rejection of the night, Doll Face left tight-lipped.

Jack was shocked and unnerved. True, the team never stayed out late or for more than a light beer during the season, but that didn't mean they didn't pick up girls on the way. It wasn't like Peter to pass on an opportunity like this.

The team left together, and they paused outside the pub in the cool night air to say goodbye and part ways. Scott and David headed down Cambridge St. with Matt and Blake, while Peter and Jack left in the opposite direction up Oxford St.

"Dude," Jack said as they walked. "That girl you blew off was hot."

"My man," Peter sighed. "She was."

"How come she's not headed home with you?"

"I have a date with Alice tomorrow."

"Oh, so now you're going exclusive?"

Peter stopped. "Sullivan, if you have a problem with me dating one of your friends, just come out with it and say so."

"I don't have a problem with you dating anyone," Jack lied. "But I care about her and I don't want to see her get hurt."

"So why did you try to fix me up with a blonde doll tonight?"

"I didn't. I was talking to her friend."

Peter ignored his lie. "Listen, my man, I get it. Alice is your friend; I told you, I have my white gloves on." He lifted his hands and wiggled his fingers. "So, did I pass the test?"

Jack nodded stiffly. Peter was too smart for his own good, only he had no idea how badly Jack wanted him to fail, not pass.

Thirteen

Alice

For her date with Peter, Alice decided to wear a long, knitted dress buttoned up at the front and ankle boots. Peter had given her his address, so at five in the evening she left her building and headed for his house. She was both excited and anxious. College guy's houses could be scary. They could range from generally unclean to sanitary service emergency. And the bathrooms… ew. The only boy's room she'd ever seen cleaner than hers was Jack's; he was too fastidious not to clean after himself. Not that it mattered. Other than for group projects, they weren't going to use his room for any extracurricular activities.

She had to stop thinking about Jack. He wasn't a variable in her sentimental equation anymore. She was going on a date with Peter, not Jack. The tall, blue-eyed team captain needed to be her sole focus. What would Peter's house be like? Alice was about to find out. She stopped in front of a mahogany wood-framed house, a duplex actually, and double checked the address before ringing the bell.

Peter came to the door wearing gray sweatpants and a white t-shirt. *Why are guys in sweatpants instantaneously ten times hotter?*

They hugged on the threshold and he showed her inside. The house smelled of eggs but in a good way. Despite this being a college-boys-inhabited apartment, the place didn't look too dirty. Not stark clean, but not gross either.

Alice followed Peter behind the kitchen bar where he had two pans on the stove.

"Mmm." She inhaled deeply. "Smells good. How come you can cook?"

"I'm part Italian on my mother's side. She taught me."

"Wow. Can you speak Italian?"

"Un po'."

"That sounds like Spanish, un poco. How about something more elaborate?"

"All right. Sei bella come il sole."

Alice recognized the word "bella." He must have paid her a compliment of some kind. Hearing him speak Italian was too thrilling to be wise. So she moved on to safer topics. "That was cool. What are you making for dinner?"

"Grazie. And I'm making spaghetti carbonara. Please tell me you're not a trouble-eater."

"Trouble-eater?"

"Yeah, you know, vegetarian, pescatarian, gluten-hater, or something like that."

"I'm not, I swear. I love pasta, and I couldn't live without bacon."

"Great, because this recipe has both. I've opened the wine if you want to pour us a glass."

Alice turned toward the bar where the opened wine bottle and glasses were. This was all very grown up. Much more of a mature date than what she would have expected from a college boy. It was the kind of date Ethan would have taken her on.

She winced at the thought of her ex. Her heart was still a bit sore from the breakup—er, *dismissal.* In the span of two weeks, her boyfriend had dumped her and her best friend had returned her romantic advances with the warmth of an ice block. If it weren't for Peter, she'd be at an all-time low. He was the perfect distraction, one that could cook delicious pasta with loads of bacon in it, judging from the smell.

Alice poured the wine—red, of course—and handed Peter a glass. "So, you live here alone?"

"No, I have a roommate. He's visiting his family this weekend, and he doesn't have classes on Monday, the lucky bastard," Peter said. "He'll be back tomorrow night."

Leaving them alone in the house for the entire evening. *Well-played.* Alice wasn't sure if she wanted to sleep with Peter tonight. As dates went, it was so far so good, but her mind wasn't made up yet. She decided to go with the flow and see where the evening would lead.

Alice didn't comment on the *Home Alone* situation, so she just lifted her glass and said, "Cheers." She clinked her glass against his and they both took a sip.

Peter started working on the sauce while Alice hovered behind him. He bent over a bowl beating raw eggs with a fork and mixing them with some kind of grated cheese. Watching him cook made him sexier than usual. He still hadn't kissed her, although she wished he would.

He lifted the lid off the stockpot, probably to check if the water was boiling, which it was. Then he threw some salt in, followed by the spaghetti, set a timer on his phone, and turned to her.

"Did you enjoy the game last night?" he asked.

"Actually, I did."

"You seem surprised."

"I am a bit. I thought sports were boring, but when you have a team to cheer for, it's exhilarating." She beamed at him. "Congratulations on the win."

Peter shrugged. "Thanks. We didn't play at our best, though, and the season is long."

"Madison said Harvard was a bit on the cheap side, as basketball pavilions go."

"She's right," Peter agreed, surprising Alice. "But a degree from Harvard is a degree from Harvard. There's no topping that."

"So you chose a better school with a less-than-stellar team?"

"Yeah, basically."

"Even if you're shooting for the NBA?" Alice asked.

"Scouts will spot talent no matter the team you play on, and I could get a serious injury at any point in my career. A good degree never goes away."

Peter was proving to be more levelheaded than she'd expected.

"Cheers to that," Alice said, taking another sip of wine.

Peter checked the timer. "The pasta will be ready in a minute," he said, and came closer to her. She was leaning with her back against the kitchen bar, and he trapped her between it and his body. He set his glass on the bar, took hers away, and put it down next to his. "Which means I have exactly sixty seconds left to kiss you."

He wrapped his arms around her back and pressed his lips to hers. Alice's entire body warmed, an electric current spreading through her from head to toe. When the beeping timer put an end to the kiss, Alice wished pasta took longer to cook.

"You can sit down," Peter said, pointing her toward the table. "I'll bring the pasta over in a second."

Alice noticed the laid table for the first time. The living area was an open space that included the kitchen, the main living room, and a small dining area on the side. The table setting wasn't too fancy, but, again, impressive for an alleged college jock.

"Mmm, this is delicious," Alice said after tasting the first forkful of spaghetti. "You have to give me the recipe."

Peter shook his head, smiling. "Not possible. If you want real Italian pasta, you'll have to come to me."

Was he planning another date already? "You mean you want me to knock on your door whenever I'm craving great pasta?" she teased. "That could become a problem."

"With you, it wouldn't be."

Bit cheesy, but Alice let it slide, accepting the compliment. A girl could get used to wonderful homemade dinners and a stream of compliments coming from a smoking hot, tall guy in sweatpants.

"I haven't made any dessert," Peter said once they'd finished eating the pasta.

"Oh, that's all right." Alice patted her belly. "I'm already so full."

"Want to finish the wine on the couch?"

Heat rose in her cheeks. She was certain the couch was heavy-making-out territory. "Sure."

Peter emptied the bottle into their glasses and picked them both up, guiding the way to the living room. They sat almost on top of each other, her legs across his lap, her back leaning against the puffy couch arm. They chatted a little longer, Peter casually stroking her shins as they talked. Her head was spinning a little—because of the wine, or because of Peter, she couldn't tell.

I like him, she realized. *A lot.* The night they'd met, their first date, and now tonight—everything with him was perfect, exciting, new. Peter wasn't the superficial jerk Jack insisted he was.

Jack. She didn't want to think about him or her unrequited love for him ever again. Alice wanted to close that book and move onto a much more interesting read.

When her glass was empty, Peter took it from her and set it on the coffee table. He pulled her fully onto his lap and they started kissing. After a while, he flipped them over and laid her on the cushions, pressing his body on top of hers. That's when Alice knew they weren't simply going to make out and then say goodnight—she was aching for more, and she could tell he was too. Peter was an amazing kisser, and her toes curled as she imagined what he would do to her in a bed.

Alice tried to stay in the moment and not think what it'd feel like if it was Jack on top of her. She needed to move on with her life. She was too old to believe in fairytales; time to grow up. Ethan, Jack… they were her past. Peter was her present.

Fourteen

Jack

Jack wanted to kill someone. A very specific someone. Sulking, he watched Alice walk into their first Monday class with her cheeks flushed from the cold and a dreamy smile on her lips—she was practically *glowing*. Peter hadn't given Jack any specifics at practice, which was the first red flag. But his smug, stupid face and confident smirk had hinted at more than enough for Jack to figure out that his captain had gotten lucky with Ice.

They'd slept together. Jack had no doubts. The thought was like a sucker punch to his guts. He was rotten jealous; there was no denying it at this point. He'd always thought he was fine with Alice being his friend and nothing more, a platonic relationship. *Wrong*. When she'd tried to kiss him, something had stirred in him, and seeing her with Peter was torture. Thinking of them together turned his stomach in a washing machine spinning at full speed.

For the first time, Jack had arrived at a lecture before Alice. He was usually late as he had to run all the way across campus from the gym after practice. Today, he'd managed to get in at the top of the hour and Alice was fifteen minutes late. *Ice was never late.* Had Peter given her such mind-blowing sex that she'd had trouble getting up this morning? Jack's stomach churned again.

What now? Should he tell her? Tell her what, exactly? Accuse her of having had sex with Peter? Demand an explanation? Or go for something more along the lines of,

"*Hey, Ice, remember the other day when you tried to kiss me and I told you it wasn't going to happen between us because we're just friends? I was kidding. Let's get together.*"

She would laugh in his face. Coming clean with her now would be a disaster, and Jack still wasn't sure starting a relationship with Ice was right. What if he screwed up again? He'd already lost one best friend because he'd thought he was in love with Felicity when he wasn't. He'd mistaken familiarity and attraction for something they weren't. Was he misinterpreting plain territorial jealousy for deeper feelings here? Jack didn't know what he felt for Alice or if he should be with her; the only clear certainty in his mind was that she shouldn't be with Peter.

If he'd never cared who Alice dated before, why the change now? What if Alice wasn't the problem? Maybe it was Peter. Jack didn't like his captain invading his turf. Yeah, that must've been it. Male competition was his problem, not his non-existing-before-two-weeks-ago feelings for Ice. Jack had better play it cool with both of them. Their relationship would evaporate just like all the other relationships Peter had. He shouldn't worry. This problem would solve itself.

Still, when Alice sat next to him and uttered a cheerful, "Hey!" Jack felt like punching something—no, some*one*.

"Hi," he replied stiffly. "Had a good weekend?"

"Yeah. You?"

"Just the usual: practice, game, homework."

"Yeah, I saw the game. It was, uh, cool."

"I played like crap."

"The team won; it's all that matters."

"Yeah, scoring is all that usually matters with basketball players."

He noticed Alice stiffen in her chair.

"Are you having a bad morning?" she asked.

"You could say that." Jack sneered. "For one, it started with me having to listen to Peter bragging about scoring with you."

"He did *what?*" Alice hissed. "Did he tell the entire team we had sex?"

Jack felt as if he'd just been punched in the stomach. *So I was right—it did happen.* He wanted to lie to her and claim Peter had gone bragging to everyone—what better way to drive a wedge in their relationship?—but he couldn't bring himself to do it. "No, he just told me," Jack admitted. "Actually, he didn't say it—but I can read between the lines. Thank you for the confirmation."

Alice blushed. She hid her face by bending forward to take her notepad out of her messenger bag.

"So how was it?" Jack asked. He couldn't help his morbid curiosity.

"You've never asked me about sex with other guys before," Alice whispered.

"You've never dated any of my friends before."

"Oh, so that gives you kiss-and-tell privileges?" She scowled at him. "I don't think so."

"If it sucked, you can just say it."

"No, it didn't suck. It was the best sex of my life," Alice whispered furiously. "Happy now?"

Yeah, Jack had gotten what he wanted. He basked in the bitter satisfaction of having tricked her into saying what gave pain to no one but himself.

"Mr. Sullivan, why don't you answer the question?" Professor Procter targeted Jack. "You seem pretty busy discussing hypotheses with Miss Brown."

Luckily, Jack's subconscious had been half-following the lecture, and he was able to cook up a half-decent answer. After the rebuke, he and Alice didn't exchange another word for the rest of the class, and Jack made himself promise he would never discuss Peter with Alice ever again—especially not how good his captain was in bed.

Live and let live was truly the best solution. Jack would let Peter ruin everything on his own. No need to interfere or say anything. Peter would dig his own grave, eventually.

***

Jack's do-nothing-and-life-will-take-care-of-it plan failed miserably. Two months later, Alice and Peter were still dating. Peter had either become monogamous or was smart enough not to let Jack catch him with some other girl. To be honest, Jack really believed Peter was being faithful to Alice. What with their super-packed schedule, Jack didn't see how Peter could fit in another woman; it was nearly impossible. The thought gave him little consolation.

Besides his mood, Jack's performance on the basketball field had suffered too. Alice had become a regular presence at their home games, keeping Jack angry and distracted. Not a good combination when you were playing a team game and all you wanted to do was strangle your captain. Coach Morrison noticed something was up, but Jack refused to provide any explanation, so the coach made him play the bench more often than the court.

On top of everything else, his dating life was nonexistent. All of a sudden, women who were not Ice seemed dull to him. Jack didn't see the point in sleeping with any of them anymore. The notion that he didn't want to sleep with anyone else because of Alice surprised and scared him. The only person who knew of this turmoil was his friend Felicity. Over the phone, she'd told him—not without a hint of regret in her voice—that he'd finally fallen in love with someone. And that not wanting to sleep with anyone else because they weren't Alice was exactly what being in love felt like.

Jack didn't know what to do with this unwelcome intel on his feelings. Telling Ice now, when she already had a boyfriend, would be a stupid move. Also, the possibility that she could turn him down left him in a state of panic. Was this how Ice had felt after the library incident? Why had he been so stupid? In the last few months, Jack had relived that afternoon over and over in his head. In every single one of his fantasies, he had scooped Alice into his arms and kissed her back. How could he have been so stupid, and how could Ice have moved on so quickly?

She hadn't told him she loved him—but had she? Was her love for him over, finished, caput? Just like that? Was she in love with Peter now?

Nausea assaulted him whenever he let his mind drift in that direction. Jack needed a break. A break from seeing Alice almost every day and feeling her less close to him with every passing hour. Ice spent more and more of her free time with her boyfriend and ignored her supposed best friend. In response, Jack's ego crouched in a dark corner of his mind like a sulky child neglected by his parents.

Mercifully, winter break was approaching fast. There'd be no time for Alice and Peter to be together. The team was flying to Hawaii over Christmas to play three games in Honolulu. No way would Peter behave himself on a trip where they'd be surrounded by hulu beauties 24-7. *No. Way.*

Fifteen
Alice

Alice and Peter were in the library, heads bent over their respective coursework. It was the weekend before finals week and, for once, Peter didn't have any games to play or prep for. Not that it helped their dating schedule much. Whatever time could be spared from basketball, Peter had to dedicate to revisions. Hence, their "romantic" library date.

Alice stared at her textbook, trying to take in the complex formulas of molecular orbital theory but not really succeeding. She felt guilty for being here with Peter. She'd always done her last minute revisions with Jack, but lately, they didn't hang out much outside classes.

Jack had stopped antagonizing her about her relationship with Peter, and she'd stopped asking him about his dates. She didn't want to know anymore, and he was being uncharacteristically discreet. He hadn't bragged about a new girl in a while. Not that Alice kidded herself into thinking he had not boasted because he had nothing to boast about. Alice didn't know if she felt better or worse not knowing exactly what was going on in Jack's love life. Yet, a new stubbornness compelled her to never ask.

Alice had asked Jack if he wanted to join them for this study session, but he had replied with a curt, "No, thanks!" that had sounded more like "I'd rather walk on broken glass barefooted."

Peter looked up from his econometrics book and asked, "Are you going home for Christmas?"

"No. Every year my parents go on a cruise for Christmas." Alice grimaced. "Be away on the 25th and you can get the cheapest fares ever. My family is more about Thanksgiving. I'll stay here and get a head start on spring term."

"Alone on Christmas Day?" Peter arched his brows. "That's sad."

Alice shrugged. "I'm used to it."

"Why don't you come to Hawaii?"

That had been her latest discovery about the Harvard basketball team. The Crimson weren't free, not even for Christmas. They had to fly to Hawaii to play three games, one of which was on the 25th. Okay, there were worse fates than "having" to go to Hawaii at Christmas time. But still…

"Hawaii?" Alice repeated.

"Yeah, why not?" Peter stared at her expectantly. "We leave on the 21st and we get back on the 26th. I know we have three games, but they usually leave us some chill time in between. My parents can't make the trip, so it'll be just the two of us."

"And the team." *And Jack.*

"Yeah, but I can cut some free time, and it's a week in Maui." Peter's enthusiasm was evident. "It's better than staying here buried under the snow, alone on Christmas Day."

"Yeah, but you'd be busy most of the time with the team, no?"

"True," he admitted. "Why don't you ask your roommates along? You girls could go sunbathing on the beach when I have team duty, and we could hang out the rest of the time."

Alice considered the possibilities. "Madison has to go home at Christmas for sure. Her family's a bit overbearing. But I could ask Haley." Christmas in Hawaii was starting to sound like a real option. "Are you seriously asking me to go to Hawaii with you?"

"Never been more serious."

Alice chewed her pen. "Can I think about it?"

"What is there to think about?" Peter mimicked hula dancing. "What could be better than flying to a tropical beach with your awesome boyfriend?"

Boyfriend. So far, Alice had thought of their relationship as hanging out or casual dating, but Peter had just made it official.

"I can't say yes for sure," Alice conceded. "I have to check flight fares and ask Haley if she can come."

Alice was stalling to gain some time to decide. The truth was, every year since she'd moved to Boston, her parents had given her a very generous Christmas gift, basically a bribe, to appease the guilt of not spending the day with her. She had saved up the money for the past two years—but maybe, for once, she could stop being super responsible and give herself a break. A Hawaiian break.

Alice was both thrilled and wary of Peter's proposal. True, sports could be fun to watch. Yet, whenever the team lost—a fifty-fifty chance so far—Peter became sulky and short-tempered. It could be hard to be near him after a lost game. Jack was a tad less moody about it, but basketball wasn't as important for him.

To be honest, it felt like basketball was the third wheel in her relationship with Peter. It was an all-consuming element in Peter's life with practice almost every day and several games a week, both at home and in other cities. Before, being Jack's friend but not taking a real interest in the game, Alice hadn't noticed how demanding it was.

She had a love-hate relationship with basketball now. Watching Peter play—okay, she kept an eye on Jack too, she couldn't help it—was exhilarating. It was like dating someone in a band. Whenever you put a man on a stage of sorts, it was guaranteed women would find him instantly more attractive. For Peter, it was exactly like that. On the field, he had a huge spotlight on him that made him irresistible. And he wanted to spend Christmas with her.

Christmas in Hawaii with Peter sounded awesome in theory. But what if the team lost? She'd be in a tropical paradise with her boyfriend and a dark cloud of bad temper over their heads. *Not ideal.* Also, it wasn't going to be a cheap or short trip. But if Haley could go, it'd be a fun trip, better than staying in an empty campus during the Christmas holidays. As gorgeous as Harvard was, it wasn't Hogwarts.

When she thought about it that way, the choice was clear. It was between Hawaii with Peter and possibly one of her best friends—two, counting Jack—or Cambridge alone. Mmm. Last year, Madison had invited her to celebrate with her family. Every year, the Smithsons had this huge Christmas celebration at their country house. It had been such a cheery, fuzzy-warm day. And also the day she'd met Ethan. Madison would invite her again, but Alice couldn't accept this time; it'd be too awkward. Ethan probably had no desire to have his ex sprinkled on him on Christmas Day. And what if he brought his new girlfriend? *Ugh.* It'd be a holidays nightmare.

There was no contest. She was going to Hawaii.

***

Alice barged into her apartment barely able to contain her excitement. "Roommates meeting!" she announced.

Haley and Madison were seated at the dining table revising for finals. Madison was studying poetry verses, and Haley code lines. They both lifted their heads, looking grateful for the interruption.

"What's up?" Haley asked, sagging on the couch.

Madison sat next to Haley, and Alice chose the armchair on the side. "Peter's invited me to go to Hawaii with him over Christmas," she said. "The team has to play three games there, and he wants me to go."

"Hawaii? Wow." Haley seemed excited.

Alice beamed. "Would you girls like to come with me?"

Madison's face fell. "I can't go," she said at once. "You know how my family is about Christmas and traditions. I can't skip it."

Alice had expected that. "Haley?"

"How many days would we be there?"

"Less than a week."

"I would have to tell my parents I'm not going home for Christmas and ask them for an expense contribution," Haley said. Then, turning toward Madison, she added, "They're more flexible about holidays than your parents."

"Lucky you," Madison muttered, paling. She gave the impression of swallowing a lump in her throat.

"I'll check with my parents." Haley got to her feet and disappeared into her room.

Madison got up as well. "I have some reading to do," she said, somewhat deflated. She picked up a book and disappeared into her bedroom.

Alice followed her and knocked on her door. "Can I come in?"

"Yes," came Madison's muffled voice from within.

Alice opened the door and leaned against the threshold. "I need to ask you a favor." Alice thought of the first excuse for following Madison. "Can you take care of Blue while I'm gone?"

"Sure, I'll only be gone for Christmas day."

"Thanks." Alice walked into the room. "Are you okay?"

"Yeah," Madison said a small voice. "Why?"

"You seem upset about Hawaii." Alice sat on the bed next to Madison. "What is it?"

"Nothing. I just thought you were coming to my house again for Christmas." Madison crossed her arms over her chest. "I know I haven't officially asked you yet, but I thought it was implicit."

"Yeah, I know, and thank you." Alice smiled, tight-lipped. "But I can't come to your house this year."

"Why?"

"You know why. Ethan will be there. It'd be too awkward for the both of us."

Madison grimaced and theatrically swatted her forehead with her hand. "You're right. I'm so stupid. I hadn't even thought about it."

"Are you sure there's nothing else?" Alice insisted. Madison was very private about her feelings—she had to have information like this dragged out of her.

"Like what?"

"Is it about that guy, mmm, what was his name?"

"What guy?"

"Number 23, the one you recognized at the game."

"Scott? What does he have to do with anything?"

"He's in your concentration, and I got the impression you had a little crush on him."

"I don't," Madison said, too defensive.

"Haley seemed to like him too," Alice pressed. "You wouldn't be worried about something happening between them while we're in Hawaii, then?"

Madison blushed. "No!"

"Madison, if you like him, just tell Haley he's off-limits."

"As if it would matter." Madison sulked. "If Haley Thomas wants him, she's going to get him. She doesn't even try, and all the guys love her. Nothing I say would make a difference. It's not like he's my boyfriend or anything. I've never said more than 'hello' to him."

"But if you told Haley—"

"No! And promise me you won't say anything to her about it, *ever.*"

"Why?"

"Just promise me," Madison said with an anguished face. "Can you?"

"Okay, I promise."

Alice had a hunch she'd just made a mistake. Secrets ruined friendships; nothing good could come out of this one.

Haley barged into the room a second later. "Guess what?"

"What?" Madison asked.

"My parents okayed the Hawaiian trip and, as a Christmas present, they're helping me pay for it."

"That's wonderful," Alice said.

She turned to Madison to study her reaction. Her friend was smiling, but her eyes were sad.

"Come on." Haley, oblivious as always to most of the things happening around her, grabbed Alice's hand to pull her up from the bed. "We have to plan our trip."

Alice stood up and followed Haley out of the room, throwing a dismayed Madison a wistful glance as she closed the door.

Sixteen

Alice

"Hey, Ice," Jack called, running after her at the end of their last final before winter break.

"Hey." Alice stopped walking and waited for him. "How did you do?" she asked, referring to their Organic Chemistry test.

"Good, I think." He frowned. "Except for question two, maybe. Which of the functional groups did you mark as susceptible to nucleophilic attack? A and B, or A, B, and C?"

"Just A and B."

"Great, me too." He smiled. "How about you? Any doubts?"

"Question four: the most acidic compound was CH3SH, right?" It had taken her ten minutes to mark that answer. "I always confuse them."

"Yep, that's the one."

Alice let out a relieved breath. "I should be good then."

"What do you say to a hot chocolate to celebrate? Deal?"

"Deal."

Jack was in a bright mood for a change. Since she'd started dating Peter, it had been a rare thing, and Alice missed their easygoing interactions. Given the freezing December temperatures, they headed for the nearest place: a cozy coffee shop called Crema Café. Even the short walk outside was enough to turn Alice's nose and sans-gloves hands red, so she welcomed the puff of warm air that blasted her as she pushed into the coffee shop.

The atmosphere inside, besides being deliciously warm, was also incredibly festive. Red and white Christmas decorations rested on every available surface, and the crowd was loud and cheerful. At four in the afternoon on the last day of finals, pretty much the whole campus was on vacation.

"Grab a table," Jack said. "I'll go order. Chocolate with cream?"

"Yeah." Alice uncoiled her scarf from around her neck. "Medium, please."

"I'll be right back."

Jack scurried off to join the line and Alice couldn't avoid noting how well his pants fitted him. *Bad Alice,* she chided herself, *no more checking out Jack's butt.* She had a boyfriend, one with a derriere just as good as Jack's. Alice had to keep drilling it into her head that she and Jack were just friends. And friends didn't ogle each other's butts. Definitely not.

The only free table was a tiny one in the back that barely seated two. Alice removed her coat, sat down, and waited for Jack while blowing into her cupped hands to warm them. The hot paper cup Jack handed her five minutes later did a much better job of heating her frozen fingers.

"I'm so glad this semester is over," Jack announced, plonking down on the chair next to her.

Close. *Too* close. Despite the place being crowded and the cocoa aroma drifting up from her cup, Alice could still smell Jack's aftershave. It made her stomach contract a bit, so she flooded it with hot chocolate to force her belly to relax.

"Yeah, me too," she said. "This one was hard; not that I've encountered an easy one yet." Alice was babbling. They had spent a million afternoons just like this one. There was no reason to be this nervous. "We should put vodka in this." Alice shook the cup. "It's so vanilla of us to celebrate with chocolate."

"I have a game soon," Jack said matter-of-factly. "Nothing stronger than beer for me."

Alice felt a stab of annoyance. "I should change best friends. You're not daring enough."

Jack's eyes sparkled. He gave her a look that said, "Try me." A hot, red flush crept its way up from Alice's neck to her cheeks. They held each other's gaze for a second longer before the moment was lost. Jack's head disappeared under the table as he retrieved something from his bag.

"To overcome my shortcomings in the fun department," Jack said once his torso was straight again, "I got you something for Christmas."

Alice stared wide-eyed at the tube-shaped bundle he was holding. "Are we doing presents now?"

They'd never given each other gifts before.

"Nah. It's really nothing." Jack shrugged. "I saw it in a shop window the other day and it made me think of you…"

"Can I open it now, or do I have to wait for Christmas Day?"

Jack flashed her a grin. "Go ahead."

Alice attacked the wrapping paper. It came off to reveal a cute pink bunny shape.

"What is this?"

"If you remove the case it becomes an umbrella," Jack said, his voice hesitant.

Alice's heart stopped. She stared at the pink umbrella covered in tiny white dots, unable to lift her gaze to meet Jack's eye.

"I know it's silly," Jack continued. He sounded just as nervous. "But do you remember that night—"

Alice lifted her gaze and locked eyes with Jack. "Of course I remember…"

***

It was a stormy spring night, with rain pouring from the sky by the bucket. Jack and Alice were waiting for Jack's girlfriend to come out of the pub where they'd all had dinner. The atmosphere inside the pub had been humid and suffocating. So much so that when the girlfriend—whatever her name was—had needed to use the restroom, Alice and Jack had preferred to wait outside in spite of the rain. Since that first awful dinner with Olivia, it had become routine for Jack to bring his dates along from time to time when he and Alice went out together.

They took shelter under the pub's ledge, Jack standing in front of her near the door. After a couple of minutes, the door was pushed open, forcing Jack to squeeze her between his chest and the pub wall to keep out of the downpour. Too close. With her back to the wall and Jack looming over her, Alice's skin prickled. Embarrassed, she shifted to the side, keeping under the ledge, making it look as if they weren't together. A bulky guy with a black umbrella came out of the pub. He did a quick scan of the road and focused his attention on Alice.

"Hey, you," bulky guy said. "Bad night to go home without an umbrella. Want a spot under mine?"

Before Alice could do or say anything, he grabbed Alice by the waist, pulling her close to him. His breath reeked of onion rings and beer. It made Alice gag.

"I'm good, thanks," Alice said, trying and failing to push him away. He had her in a viselike grip and wouldn't let go.

"Come on," Mr. Bad-breath said, sending another wave of foul stench her way. "I'm taking you home." He started dragging her down the road.

Jack's deadly-cold voice came from behind them. "She said she's fine."

Mr. Bad-breath stopped. "What's your problem, dude?" He turned toward Jack. "Is she your girlfriend?"

"No, she's not," Jack replied, his voice low.

At the look of controlled fury on Jack's face, the guy tried to justify himself. "I was only offering her space under my umbrella."

"She already has an umbrella," Jack said.

"I don't see any umbrella," the guy protested.

Jack wrenched Alice free. "I'm her fucking umbrella," he growled, shoving Mr. Bad-breath away. A look of furious determination darkened his eyes.

"Whatever, dude." Mr. Bad-breath walked away from a fight he was certain to lose given the resolve in Jack's eyes, leaving them both standing in the rain.

Alice's hair and clothes were getting soaked, but she didn't care. She lifted her gaze to Jack. "That was very Rihanna of you," she said to smooth the tension.

Jack's jaw relaxed, and he flashed her half a smile. Neither of them moved; they just stood there in the pouring rain, staring into each other's eyes. The way he was looking at her made Alice's pulse speed up. He moved a step closer. Oh, gosh, was he going to kiss her?

"Jack!" his girlfriend called. "What are you doing in the rain?" Whatever-her-name-was came and stood next to him, placing him under the shelter of her own umbrella.

Alice was the only one left standing in the rain, her hair and clothing drenched. And her role in the scene shifted from movie-romantic to incredibly pathetic in an instant.

"I guess I'll get going," Alice said. "I'm only a block away." More like four or five.

She spun around, not waiting for a reply, although she did manage to catch the death stare whatever-her-name-was flashed her. Then she hurried off into the rain, not daring to look back and catch Jack's eye.

***

Alice thanked Jack for the bunny-themed gift and managed to nod her way through the rest of the conversation in the time it took them to finish their hot chocolates.

When a solid, minute-long silence lingered between them, she said, "We should get going."

"Well," Jack said, getting up to leave. "Seeya after Christmas." He grabbed his bag from the floor.

Alice got up as well. "Mmm, about that." She wasn't sure why telling Jack she was going to Hawaii was making her so nervous. But she couldn't put it off any longer. "We might see each other sooner than that."

"I'm flying to Hawaii tomorrow, Ice. No chance."

"I know. But when I told Peter I was alone for Christmas, he invited me to Hawaii." She smiled half-heartedly. "So Haley and I are going."

Jack's face fell, sending a chill up both of her arms.

"Don't be too excited," Alice said.

"It's not… I mean," he stuttered, eyes wide with surprise. "You're coming to Hawaii?"

"I am."

"That's great."

His creased forehead and tight-lipped smirk sent a completely different message from "great."

"I'll see you at the airport tomorrow," Alice added, annoyed, but trying not to show it. "We're on the same flight."

"Of course."

Now Jack looked as if he was standing on hot coals. He shifted his weight from foot to foot and seemed eager to get away from her as quickly as possible.

"Well, I'll catch you tomorrow then." Jack took two steps backward. "Gotta go. Bye." He turned on his heel and was gone before Alice had a chance to add anything.

Outside, it had started snowing. Fat, feathery flakes were spiraling down, coating the streets in white frost. Alice shook her head and opened her new umbrella to walk home.

Seventeen

Haley

The Uber driver dropped Haley and Alice off at Logan International Airport super early the next morning. Haley fidgeted all the way through the airline check in and airport security checks. Since they were leaving so early, they had skipped breakfast at home. And Haley was starving. When they finally stopped at a Starbucks near their gate to grab a quick bite, her stomach was already grumbling in protest.

As Haley sipped her grande caffè mocha, a tall guy shuffling through the Hudson News shop across the hall caught her attention. He had his back turned so she couldn't see his face, only his clothes. He was wearing sweatpants and a puffy sports jacket with a hoody pulled over his head.

"Hello?" Alice asked next to her. "Are you listening?"

"No, sorry, I was distracted by the hottie over there."

"Which one?"

"The one in the puffy blue jacket?"

"How can you say he's hot? I can only see his back."

"It's a hot back. I wish he'd turn around." She stared at his shoulders, whispering, "Turn, turn…"

Both Haley and Alice followed the mysterious guy's progress around the shop, but he walked away without once turning his face toward them.

"Aw, pity," Haley said. "Now we'll never know."

Alice rolled her eyes. "I think I'll live."

"That's because you already have a hot boyfriend. We single gals, on the other hand…"

"Need to ogle strangers in airports?" Alice offered.

"Pretty much." Haley laughed.

"So you're definitely over your masked stranger?"

Haley's heart gave a wistful pulse. Last summer she'd gone to a Venetian Masquerade Ball and danced with a masked stranger only to lose him halfway through the night and never see him again. She'd been a bit obsessed ever since. She'd never even seen his face, making the search that much harder. But her mask had been a simple rhinestones application around her eyes that left her face practically bare, so she'd hoped that if she couldn't find him, he would somehow find her. But that had been months ago, and she'd lost faith.

"Not much of a choice," Haley said, "I have to use the restroom. Wait for me here?"

Haley left without waiting for a reply. She searched the ceiling for the restrooms signs and followed them to the Ladies' Room. As she pushed open the door, it banged into someone.

"Oh, sorry," she apologized.

An older woman scowled at her. Haley poked her head inside and saw the room was packed with people waiting in line. There were only four stalls, and one of them was out of order. It'd take her forever to wait for her turn. *Why are women's restrooms always so busy?* The thought gave her an idea. She backtracked from the Ladies' Room and decided to scout out the situation in the Men's Room.

Haley stopped in front of the Men's Room door. She checked behind her shoulders. *All clear.* It was empty inside, and all the stall doors were open. *Go figure.* Haley snuck into the room and went about her business as quickly as possible, rushing outside as soon as she was finished.

Just when she thought she'd made it undetected, Haley bumped into someone on her way out. She found her gaze level with a puffy blue jacket. *The guy from the news shop.* Haley had to bend her neck backward to see his face: green eyes, chiseled features, and a cute smile. He was so tall and *so* hot. Recognition gnawed at her. Where had she seen him before?

The hot guy stepped back. "Pardon me," he said, double-checking that he had the right restroom. "Isn't this the Men's Room?"

"Yeah, sorry," Haley apologized, embarrassed. "There was a super long line for the Ladies' Room, and here was empty, so..." Haley kept looking at his gorgeous face, trying to place it. "I'm sorry, have we met before?" And now she'd just used the oldest pickup line in the book. Great.

"I think I'd remember meeting you." His lips curled upwards in an amused smile. He kept his eyes trained on hers, making her blush. "We could've crossed paths on campus." He jerked his chin toward her Harvard sweatshirt. "I go to Harvard too."

"Going home for Christmas?"

"No, actually. I'm on the basketball team and we're going to Hawaii to play."

That was it! She'd seen him at a game.

"Really?" Haley couldn't believe her luck. "Me too."

He arched his eyebrows. "You play basketball for the Crimson?"

"No." Haley laughed awkwardly. "What I meant was that my best friend is dating your captain, and he's invited her along, so we're going to Hawaii with the team, sort of."

His smile widened. "Small world."

Haley tilted her head to the side. "So it seems."

"It was nice meeting you…?"

"Haley Thomas."

"Scott Williams."

He looked at her expectantly, and Haley realized she was still blocking his path to the Men's Room. They both moved at the same time, bumping into each other again. They did a little dance of moving in the same direction twice before Scott stopped and allowed Haley to move past him. She started toward the café, but couldn't help turning back. Scott was holding the door open, watching her go.

Haley smiled and ran off, eager to tell Alice the news.

Eighteen
Alice

Alice's heart jolted in fear as Haley pounced on her from behind.

"Guess what?" Haley asked, with a smile so big it shined like a lighthouse beacon.

"What?"

"I bumped into Mr. Hot-Back in the restrooms. Alice, he's so gorgeous I could barely stand to look at him without melting. And it gets better." Haley paused for effect. "He's a player for the Crimson; we'll be in Hawaii together for the next week." Haley gave a high-pitched giggle, making Alice flinch. "How unbelievable is that? I mean, it must've been destiny or something, right?"

An ominous feeling of dread wrapped itself around Alice's stomach. "What was his name?" she asked in a flat voice.

"Scott."

Alice's face fell. Why of the twenty guys—okay, eighteen minus Jack and Peter—on the team did Haley have to like the same one Madison liked?

Haley's bright smile faltered. "Please stop. You're overwhelming me with your enthusiasm," she complained. "Something bad I should know about this guy?"

Alice considered breaking her promise to Madison. Instead, she resigned herself to being a passive spectator to this Haley-Scott disaster in the making. "No, not at all," she said. "I know nothing about him, and neither do you."

"I don't need to know anything besides the fact that he's the most epically gorgeous guy I've ever seen."

Alice shrugged. "What if he's a d-bag?"

"Why do you have to be so negative?" Haley glared at her. "What's the matter with you?"

Alice was saved answering by Peter grabbing her from behind and kissing her neck.

"Yo. Here's my beautiful lady," he said.

Alice turned to say hello and instinctively tried to peek over his shoulder to see if he was with Jack. There was a group of basketball players standing nearby, but Jack wasn't with them.

"Yo, everyone," Peter continued loudly. "Meet my better half."

Better half? That was cheesy, coming from Peter. Alice wondered what had gotten into him.

Alice shook hands with the team members she didn't know and introduced Haley. Almost everyone looked at her friend as if she were a bowl of ice cream and they were a spoon. After all, Haley was the only single Crimson groupie. Alice hoped someone could still distract her from Scott.

"Scott, my man!" Peter shouted. "Over here."

Scott and Peter did that thing of clasping hands and bumping chests before Peter introduced Alice.

"Scott Williams, meet Alice Brown. Alice, meet Scott."

Alice finally understood what the Scott fuss was about. Up close, he was definitely a looker, with his dark blond hair and green eyes. Harvard might not have the fanciest basketball pavilion, but they definitely had the best-looking NCAA team.

"And this is her roommate, Haley Thomas," Peter said to Scott.

Scott flashed Haley an amused grin. "I believe we've met."

Haley blushed, astonishing Alice. Her friend never blushed. Haley and Scott immediately started talking, unaware of anything else around them. Alice was worried; both her friends liked the same guy, and it looked like one of them was going to get him. How would Madison react when they came back and told her? She would say nothing and suffer in silence, Alice suspected. *Please let Madison's crush on Scott not be serious,* she thought.

An announcement played in the background.

"Yo, guys," Peter said. "This is our flight. Let's go before the coach comes looking for us."

Peter put an arm around Alice's shoulders and steered her toward the gate.

"So, what is the policy with your coach?" she asked. "Am I allowed to be here? I mean, is it normal to invite people along?"

"Sure. I'd say about half the guys will have their families there."

"Oh, okay."

As they reached their gate and joined the boarding queue, Alice started scanning the crowds again for any sign of Jack. She couldn't spot him anywhere, which freaked her out. He *had* to be coming, so where the hell was he?

Her question found an answer as they boarded. Jack was settled in a window seat all the way to the back. He had his arms crossed over his chest, his head tilted to the side, and he was wearing a sleeping mask. *A sleeping mask?*

How could he already be on the plane, let alone asleep? Even if he'd been the first in line, he must've boarded the plane... what? Five, ten minutes ago, tops? And he knew she'd be there. So why wear the mask before they'd even said hello?

With a sinking feeling, Alice realized that Jack wearing the mask and pretending to be asleep had to be a twisted way of avoiding her. The "why" of it remained a mystery.

Was he mad at her for coming? That must be it. When she told him she was coming to Hawaii, he'd basically fled. But why? Why was it so annoying to have her here? Was it a turf invasion? A mixing of groups he didn't want to be mixed? Was he still worried about her dating Peter? He hadn't said a word about it in two months.

Well, fine then. If he wanted to ignore her the entire trip, he could suit himself. She ignored the gut-twisting spasm of annoyance in her stomach and took her seat next to Peter.

Nineteen
Jack

Under the sleeping mask, Jack squeezed his eyes shut until they hurt. He knew his little act wouldn't accomplish much, but he couldn't face Alice and Peter on their romantic trip. The idea made his stomach cramp. To avoid them completely was impossible, but Jack was determined to keep the interactions to a strict minimum. The break he'd so coveted had transformed into his worst nightmare. And a night tossing in bed dreading the next day had not helped him come to terms with the situation.

From his corner at the back of the plane, Jack listened as Peter let out his usual repertoire of "yo, oooh, my man" as he greeted everybody else. He listened as his captain introduced Alice to the players who didn't know her yet. A bitter tang spread under his tongue. Even the right of introducing Alice to the team had been stolen from him. He should be the one at her side making introductions, not Peter. Still brooding, Jack eavesdropped as Peter maneuvered people around so that he could sit next to Alice. *How sweet.* He wanted to throw up.

Jack kept his eyes shut under the mask and tried not to tense his jaw and mouth. Torture; it was a slow torture to lie still in his seat pretending to be asleep. He was so on edge real sleep was out of the question, even after take-off when the plane quieted down. To be wide-awake, unable to move, and with nothing to do was mentally exhausting.

He couldn't check the time on his phone, so he tried to judge by what was happening around him.

The take-off happened on time, which he learned from the captain's announcement. *Six-thirty.* After a while, there was the usual ping of the seatbelt sign being switched off. *Seven?* Only half an hour had passed, and to Jack, it seemed like an eternity. More time passed, and Jack found himself counting the seconds. When would it be safe to stop pretending he was asleep? After they served breakfast and cleared out? Yeah, that was probably his best bet.

Breakfast finally arrived. Jack heard Matt, who was sitting next to him, open a plastic bag. As Matt chewed on his snack, Jack marveled at how loud he sounded. So it was true that when deprived of one sense the others intensified. Eons later, when the flight attendants came back to take the trays away, Jack was itching to take his mask off. Yet, breakfast seemed to have stirred a lot of movement in the cabin. Many people were coming and going in the small aisle between the rows of seats. It was a mass pilgrimage to the restrooms.

At one point, Jack could've sworn he heard Alice's voice somewhere to his right hiss, "*Sleeping Beauty.*" Or maybe he'd just spent too much time inside his own head. Wasn't hearing voices the first sign of going mad?

When he couldn't take it any longer, Jack removed his mask and opened his eyes. *Phew,* he was safe, no one was looking his way or moving around. All passengers seemed engaged with a movie, a book, or they were genuinely asleep. He peeked at the clock. Nine-thirty. Three hours gone, a gazillion more to go. But so far, his avoid-them-at-all-costs plan had been a success.

A short-lived one. Once the plane landed at LAX, where they had to catch a connecting flight, there was no way Jack could avoid talking to Alice. He waited for the plane to empty, postponing the inevitable as long as possible, before he walked out.

For an instant, Jack thought everybody was gone, and he'd be Alice-and-Peter free for a little longer.

Until a hand smacked his right shoulder. "Yo, my man. What's up?" Peter asked. "Where have you been, Sullivan?"

"On the plane?" Jack shrugged.

"You're funny." Peter clearly hadn't caught the sarcasm in Jack's voice. "We're going to grab a burger for lunch. You coming?"

Jack could say he wasn't hungry, but everyone would notice he was acting weird. He'd better keep up at least a tiny bit of appearances. Ice already seemed suspicious. She was standing next to Peter, and from the way she was eyeing Jack, it was clear she wasn't happy with him. "A burger sounds great," he lied. He'd rather eat paper. "I skipped breakfast; I could eat an elephant."

"Didn't you eat on the plane?" Peter asked.

"Nah, I was sleeping when they served breakfast."

Alice scoffed.

Jack ignored her.

"A lady keep you up until the small hours?" Peter asked.

Jack shrugged, neither denying nor admitting to anything. But he accompanied the shrug with a wicked smile that let everyone assume Peter had nailed him.

"Oooh," Peter hollered. "Good for you, man."

Alice didn't comment, scoffing or otherwise.

***

Their motel in Honolulu had a two-story horseshoe layout with a rectangular pool in the middle. Jack's room was on the second floor on the right side of the U; he was sharing with Matt. After an early dinner, Coach Morrison had sent them to bed to rest before their first game the next day. Jack was ready to follow the instructions and hoped Peter would too.

Matt came into the room and collapsed onto his queen bed. "I'm toasted, man," Matt said. "Do you mind if I turn off the lights?"

"No, go ahead. I'm taking a breath of fresh air."

Jack opened the French doors and walked out onto the small patio outside. It was night, but the temperature was still well above seventy degrees. Compared to frigid Boston, this was heaven. Jack stared across the pool. Half the rooms on the other side were dark. Of the illuminated ones, many had their curtains closed. *Not Alice's room.*

It felt a bit stalkerish to spy on her as she sat chatting on the bed with Haley. But Jack couldn't stop staring. He was so relieved she wasn't with Peter, he could hula dance.

His joy didn't last long. Haley and Alice both turned their heads toward the door at the same time. They giggled, hugged, and Haley jumped off the bed. Two seconds later, Peter appeared inside the room. He pulled Alice up from the bed and started kissing her.

Acid rose in Jack's throat. He continued to watch, unable to avert his eyes as Alice pulled Peter back on the bed, where he landed on top of her, never breaking the kiss. Jack felt numb; his body refused to work. The only parts still functioning were his eyes, which were inexorably trained on the gruesome scene before him.

When Peter got to his feet to close the curtains and turn off the lights, Jack gripped the metal rail so hard his knuckles turned white. Jack had no air in his lungs. His skin was on fire. His entire body seemed to burn. This tropical paradise was his personal hell. Jack wanted to scream. He wanted to drag Peter off the bed and beat him into a pulp. But most of all, Jack wanted to be the one on top of Alice. Instead, all he could do was swallow bile.

A loud crash brought him back from his haze. Two windows down from Alice's room, the curtains of another room were shaking, and loud shouts mixed with banging noises were audible even from outside. Someone was fighting.

Jack wasn't the only one who'd heard the noise. In a matter of seconds, Alice's lights switched on and Peter opened the French doors and hopped out on the patio, struggling to get back into his jeans. His head shook left and right as he tried to determine what was going on. A surge of pure joy ran through Jack's veins at the perfectly timed interruption.

"What's going on?" Matt appeared on the patio next to him, his hair tousled and his face still sleepy. "I heard a crash."

Jack pointed at the room with the shaking curtains. "I think it came from there."

"Damn right," Matt said.

At that moment, the curtains collapsed and Matt and Jack had a clear view of what was happening inside. Two guys were wrestling on the floor while a terrified Haley was begging them to stop.

"Who's that?" Jack asked.

Matt squinted his eyes. "Looks like the Williams brothers are at it again."

A wolf whistle came from the other side of the motel. It was Peter. Matt and Jack turned to look at him.

"Guys," Peter shout-whispered. "Can you see what's happening?"

"David and Scott Williams, Captain," Matt shout-whispered back. "Two doors down from yours."

More lights were popping on in other rooms. If they wanted to avoid trouble, they had to pacify the two Williamses before the rumor of a fight reached Coach Morrison.

"I'll go check." Peter gestured toward the room. "Can you guys back me up?"

"We're on it," Matt said.

From their respective patios, Matt, Jack, and Peter all rushed in and out their rooms to go stop the Williamses. Jack knew he shouldn't be happy two of his teammates were fighting. But as he ran down the motel hall, he couldn't help but feel grateful the Williams brothers hated each other.

Twenty
Haley

Today had been the best day of Haley's life, and it was about to get better. Since bumping into Scott that morning, Haley couldn't stop smiling. They'd sat next to each other on both flights and had spent the whole journey talking. And Haley had discovered Scott wasn't just a pretty face. He was the most amazing guy she'd ever met, and she could see herself falling in love with him in the blink of an eye.

"Are you sure you're okay with swapping rooms?" Alice asked.

They were chatting on the bed in their room.

"Yeah." Haley beamed at her over-concerned friend. "More than okay."

"Isn't it a bit… mmm… quick?"

"Alice, we're going to sleep in the same room." Haley rolled her eyes. "It doesn't mean we have to have sex."

Alice put her hands forward in a defensive gesture. "I'm just saying that if you're not sure, or if you change your mind at any point, you don't have to switch with Peter." She dropped her arms. "I can see him any other night."

Peter and Scott were sharing a room and Peter, playing matchmaker, had asked for a roommate swap. Both Haley and Scott had said yes. Haley was waiting with Alice for the guys to come back from their mandatory team dinner.

"Alice, I'm sure," Haley insisted. "I haven't been this excited about a guy in forever."

"I'm just saying you can take it slow if you want to."

"And I already told you I don't plan to *sleep* sleep with Scott," Haley said. "Just sleep in the same room."

Alice looked at her skeptically.

Haley smiled wickedly. "I'm not saying it's a total hands-off situation. I sure hope there will be some kissing involved."

"Okay," Alice conceded. "Because Peter will be here soon."

Haley giggled. "Hey," she said. "You know what room they're in?"

"No. Peter's coming here, so I didn't ask," Alice said. "Didn't Scott tell you?"

"Yeah. But you know me, I forgot." Haley leaned to one side of the bed to grab the room's phone and dialed nine.

The line connected after two rings.

"Reception, how may I assist you?"

"Hello," Haley said. "Could you please tell me what room Scott Williams is in? I'm here with the Harvard Crimson."

"Mr. Williams is in room 226," the efficient voice replied. "Anything else I can do for you tonight?"

"No thanks, that'll be all." Haley hung up.

As if on cue, they heard someone knock on their door.

"This must be your prince charming," Haley said, getting up to open the door.

She let Peter in, grabbed her overnight duffel bag from the floor, and left Alice and Peter alone.

Haley walked down the hall, staring at the doors. She was in room 230, so room 226 wasn't far. Haley reached it and stared, undecided. She'd been cocky with Alice, but truthfully she was super nervous. She liked Scott so much, and she was afraid he didn't like her back with the same enthusiasm. He'd been wonderful all day, but what if he'd said yes to the room swap only to do Peter a solid? Well, it was too late to change her mind now.

Haley knocked.

A tall guy—presumably another basketball player—came to open the door. He was shirtless with only a pair of fleece pants on. His dark hair was wet as if he'd just come out of the shower. Piercing blue eyes dilated in surprise at finding Haley on his doorstep. Yet, quickly, his gaze shifted in a way that could be described only as… *predatory.*

Haley was struck silent.

"Hello, again," the guy said.

Again? Had he noticed her on the plane?

"What can I do for you?" His tone and lopsided smirk were suggestive.

"Oh, I'm s-sorry," Haley stammered. "I asked the reception for Scott Williams's room and they sent me here."

"Ah, I see." Blue eyes flashed. "They had the sense to direct you to the better Williams brother."

"You-you're Scott's b-brother?"

Why was she stuttering? This guy made her nervous.

He nodded. "David."

Haley was tempted to turn and run. "D-do you know which room Scott's staying in?"

"Were you on the plane with us today?" David asked, ignoring her question.

"Yeah."

"I didn't catch your name."

"Haley."

David casually leaned against the threshold, arms crossed on his bare chest. "So who are you? His girlfriend?"

"No, we met today."

David raised both eyebrows.

"I mean." Haley tried to think how she could make him understand the situation. "I'm here with my best friend. She's dating Peter, your captain. They wanted to share a room, so we swapped. I'm supposed to be bunking with Scott."

The smirk was back on David's face. "Interesting."

"Nothing is going on." Haley didn't know why she felt the need to explain herself to this guy. "I'm just going to sleep in Scott's room, not *sleep* with Scott."

"Well," David said, gently grabbing her hand and locking eyes with her. "If you're ever interested in doing something more exciting than sleeping…" He suddenly pulled her in closer. "You know where to find me."

"David," Scott's voice came from behind her. "Let her go."

Haley tried to free herself, but David held her firmly against his chest.

"And why would I do that?" David asked.

"Can't you see you're scaring her? I won't just stand here and let you intimidate her."

David's jaw tensed. "I don't recall needing your permission to do anything."

Haley was still struggling to push him away from her, but he was not giving an inch.

"David, back off," Scott ordered between gritted teeth.

"Or what?" David asked. He made some sort of weird move and spun Haley around so that now she had her back pressed against him as he hugged her from behind. David bent his head ever so slightly. As he kept taunting Scott, his lips almost brushed against Haley's neck. "What are you going to do, little brother?"

Scott was breathing hard. "Leave. Her. Alone," he repeated, closing his hands into tight fists.

"She's all yours," David said.

He pushed Haley toward Scott, who grabbed her shoulders to steady her.

"Are you okay?" he asked.

"Yeah," Haley lied. She wasn't digging the family drama one bit.

Scott let her go and, before she had a chance to realize what he was doing, he threw himself at his brother. Fury twisted his handsome face in an unrecognizable mask.

"What the hell is wrong with you?" Scott screamed, grabbing David by the throat and nailing him against the wall.

David threw his brother back with equal force, and the two started beating the hell out of each other. They barreled around the room, knocking over furniture as they careened toward the back of the room. They ended up crashing against the French windows with a loud bang.

Haley was crying. She was yelling at them to stop, but she was too scared to go anywhere near them. So she looked on as they kept fighting. At one point, the curtains collapsed, covering their struggling bodies so only a shaking blob of fabric was visible.

Peter came into the room, pausing briefly next to Haley. "Are you okay?" he asked.

Relief washed over her. "I'm fine. Please, just make them stop."

"I'm on it." Peter darted forward and started pulling at the curtains entangled around both brothers' limbs.

"Haley, I'm here," Alice said.

Haley turned around and launched herself at her best friend, hugging her tight.

"What happened?" Alice asked.

Haley tried to reply, but instead of words, she started sobbing so hard against Alice's shoulder she no longer could talk.

Twenty-one

Alice

Alice was trying to soothe a sobbing Haley when Jack and another guy—Matt, Alice thought was his name—flooded into the room to help Peter. Working together, the trio were finally able to pull the two struggling bodies apart. As Matt and Jack forced the wrestlers to their feet, Alice recognized one of them as Scott. He didn't look as if he was ready to stop the brawl, and neither did the other contender. Jack and Matt had to restrain them while Peter planted himself in the middle, arms spread wide to keep them apart.

"Shut the door," Peter told her. "We don't need anyone else involved."

Alice let go of Haley, who finally seemed less agitated, and went to close the door.

Scott and the other dude were still struggling to break free of their teammates, but Jack and Matt were fighting back just as hard. Scott's opponent was bare-chested, and his otherwise pale skin was blotched with red patches. He didn't seem to care or notice, being too busy glowering at Scott, whose nose was trickling blood on the carpet.

"You two calm down," Peter ordered. "We can't have Coach Morrison come in here and see you like this."

The mention of the coach seemed to calm down the two hot heads. They stopped struggling. Peter lowered his arms, still standing between them.

"Are you cool?" Peter asked.

They both nodded grudgingly, and Matt and Jack let

them go.

As soon as Matt loosened his grip on Scott, he jerked his elbow up to get free. He touched his hand to his nose to keep the bleeding in check, still glowering at the other guy. He looked ready to start fighting again. Instead, Scott turned around and left the room without saying a word.

Haley watched him go with a dismayed look on her face.

"What happened here, man?" Peter asked.

The remaining amateur boxer flattened his wet, disheveled hair back, unconcerned. He was another looker for the team, but something about his face read "mean."

"My little brother must have some anger issues," mean-good-looking guy said.

Brother? This was Scott's *brother?*

"And you wouldn't know anything about provoking him?" Matt said.

Scott's brother wiped sweat from his forehead with the back of his hand. "It's not my fault if he can't control himself."

The door opened again, and another player walked in, presumably the missing roommate.

"Whoa," he said, taking in the devastation inside his room. "What happened here?"

"Scott and David decided to play real-life *Mortal Combat,*" Jack explained.

He had not looked at Alice once since he'd walked in.

"We'd better clean this up," Peter said, looking around the room. "Luckily, it looks like nothing's broken."

"Peter," Alice said.

He paused mid-motion to look at her. "Yeah, baby?"

"It's best if I stay with Haley tonight."

Was that a satisfied smirk on Jack's face? Jack bent to straighten a capsized coffee table before Alice could be sure.

Peter walked toward her. "Sure, baby, I'll see you tomorrow." He planted a tender kiss on her forehead.

"Good night everyone," Alice said, purposely avoiding Jack's gaze.

Alice and Haley left the guys to clear up the mess and walked back to their room.

Inside, Haley slumped on her bed and covered her face with her hands.

"Care to tell me what the hell happened?" Alice asked.

"I honestly have no clue," Haley moaned.

"Were they already fighting when you got there?"

"No. Reception gave me the wrong room number." Haley hugged her knees to her chest, resting her chin on them. "They gave me *David* Williams instead of *Scott* Williams."

Alice was shocked. "That really was Scott's brother?"

"Apparently. So I knock on the wrong room and David opens the door. Then he starts acting all cocky and smug." Haley imitated a dude's voice. "*Oh, they've sent you to the better brother.*"

"Was he hitting on you?"

"Oh yeah."

"Did he get physical?"

"He sort of force-hugged me. But then Scott arrived, and they started arguing and… Well, you saw."

"Yeah, heard, too. Scary."

"It was. It looked as if they wanted to kill each other." Haley scrunched her face. "How can you hate your brother that much?"

"So Scott has some family issues, huh?" Alice tried to lighten the mood.

"Mm-hmm. I wonder what the real story is."

"Rivalry?"

"Some competition is normal between siblings," Haley said. "But those two acted as if they completely, utterly loathed each other."

"They were pretty intense," Alice admitted.

"I'm sorry I ruined your romantic night."

"Haley, you didn't do anything," Alice reassured her friend. "Seems to me it was all David's fault."

"He was being a douche," Haley agreed. "But Scott attacked him first."

"Has this changed your mind about him?"

"I don't know. It definitely wasn't a first date to remember." Haley chuckled sadly. "And him running away like that without a word. Weird, huh?"

"They say women are complicated, but guys are even stranger," Alice said. "Should we try to get some sleep?"

"Oh, no!" Haley covered her face with her hands again.

"What?"

"I dropped my overnight bag in David's room."

"I'll have Peter get it tomorrow."

"Thank you." Haley peeked at her from between her fingers. "I don't want to have to see him again."

"You need to borrow some PJs?"

"No, I have a long t-shirt in my luggage I can use."

Haley hopped off the bed to get changed, and Alice dropped her head on the pillow, feeling uneasy. She stared at the ceiling, wondering what else would go wrong on this trip.

Twenty-two
Haley

A brief but decisive knock on their door woke Haley early the next morning. She dragged herself out of bed and shuffled toward the door. She peered through the peephole and saw David waiting on the other side. Haley instinctively took a step back.

"What do you want?" she called through the door.

"Good morning, Sunshine." David's ever-mocking voice was muffled on the other side. "I come in peace to return your possessions."

Haley flattened herself against the door to check again through the peephole. David wasn't lying; he had her duffel bag with him. She opened the door.

"How did you know it was mine?" she asked.

"I doubt any of my teammates wear lacy underwear, at least that I know of." David's smug smirk was infuriating. "By the way, impeccable taste."

"Give it back." Haley stretched her arm forward to grab her bag, but David snatched it backward.

"Ah, ah, ah. Not yet," he said, still smiling. "You're going to have to hear me out first."

Haley crossed her arms and took a step back. "Hear out what?"

"I wanted to apologize for what happened last night; it wasn't my intention to cause trouble."

"Yeah, it was." Haley was not about to let his charm fool her. "Why else would you be like that?"

"Well. When an amazingly beautiful girl, who is *not* my brother's girlfriend, happens to knock on my door in the middle of the night, I find it hard not to present her with…" David paused. "Options."

The compliment, no matter how cheesy, made Haley blush. Flattery rarely worked on her, but pair it with piercing blue eyes and uncanny good looks, and it did have an effect.

"Listen," Haley sighed, "I'm not sure what's going on between you and your brother, but I'm not getting in the middle of that."

"Might be too late for that."

"How so?"

"I've my heart set on you now." His blue gaze was intense and unsettling.

"Not going to happen," Haley snapped.

David winked. "Never say never."

"Can I have my bag now?"

David handed it over. "Until next time."

Without waiting for her reply, he turned on his heel and walked back to his room. For reasons inexplicable to her, Haley watched him go and waited until he disappeared into his room before she closed the door.

"Who was that?" Alice asked from her bed.

"David Williams."

Alice straightened with a worried expression. "What did he want?"

"To give my bag back and apologize for last night." Haley sat on her bed.

"Was it okay?"

Haley considered the question. “I don’t know; with him, it’s hard to say,” she admitted. “I don’t know if he was serious or if he was mocking me. Maybe he just wants to piss off his brother more.”

“Well, it was nice of him to apologize.”

“It felt more conniving than nice.”

“I could ask Peter what the deal is with the Williams brothers,” Alice offered. “No one seemed surprised they were fighting last night.”

Another knock came at the door.

“Who is it now?” Haley asked the ceiling.

“I’ll place my money on the other Williams brother.”

Haley instinctively checked herself out in the wardrobe mirror, fluffed her hair, and opened the door.

“Hi, is this a bad time?” Scott said.

“No, I was already up.”

“Hey.” He lowered his gaze to the floor, embarrassed. “I wanted to apologize for the disappearing act last night.”

“It’s okay,” Haley lied. “You don’t have to explain anything.”

“Actually, I do.” Scott looked back up. “Team duties start in little over an hour. I was wondering if you wanted to take a walk down the beach with me first?”

Scott was so genuine and sweet. Exactly the opposite of his brother.

“I would love to,” Haley said. “Can you give me fifteen minutes to get ready?”

Scott’s face brightened. “I’ll wait for you in the hall.”

***

The sand was cool this early in the morning. Haley had taken her flip-flops off and was walking barefoot on the beach. The sun was still low above the horizon, but its warm rays indicated the temperature would rise soon enough. Scott hadn't said much yet; he had a serious frown and the face of someone thinking too much.

Haley decided to break the ice first. "So that was your brother, huh?"

Scott was still lost in his thoughts. "Yep."

"What's the deal with you two?"

"We were never close." Scott looked straight ahead, his voice emotionless. "But I'm not sure when David started hating me. Maybe he thinks I've stolen his thunder or something by, you know, being born."

"Mmm, so nothing else got stolen between you two?" Haley asked.

"Ah." Scott scratched the back of his head. "Is it that obvious?"

"Well, you saw us talk last night and lost your mind. All that rage wasn't about me."

"No, you're right," Scott admitted. "It was déjà vu."

They walked a little further in silence.

"So are you going to tell me about the girl?" Haley asked when she couldn't hold it in any longer.

Scott didn't try to deny it. "It was a long time ago, in high school. Her name was Brigitte. She was a student from France doing her junior year in the US. Long story short, we both liked her, and she did something David will never forgive me for."

"What?"

"She chose me." Scott stared at the sky.

"That's it?" Haley thought there was a lot more Scott was holding back.

"No, it's a lot more complicated." He finally looked at her. "But enough about the past." He stopped to face her. "What happened yesterday won't happen again. I won't lose control like that... What I'm saying is, I'm sorry you had to see that, and I hope I haven't scared you off for good." He raised both his eyebrows in a cute and interrogative way.

Haley smiled. "You haven't... scared me off."

"Good," Scott said. "Because I've been dying to do this since the moment I first saw you." He cupped her face with his hands and lowered his mouth to hers.

Twenty-three

Alice

Christmas Day was the weirdest. It wasn't just the warm weather and floral décor that clashed with Alice's snowy image of the holiday, or that she had to eat a light, quick lunch because the team played later that night. It was being with Jack without really being with him. It felt strange, wrong. She'd always imagined their first Christmas together under different circumstances.

Alice's mood wasn't exactly cheery to begin with. Peter had seriously downplayed how much the team-related activities would keep him busy. If Alice had come alone, she'd have been pissed. Add the fight between David and Scott, the room swap complications, the fact that Jack had been a total bitch the entire time, and there was a distinct lack of *merry* in her Christmas vacation. And it was about to get worse.

The referee blew his whistle three times, signaling the end of the game. Alice stared at the scoreboard, downcast. Harvard had lost. They'd won their first two games, and Alice had hoped the winning streak would continue. But no. Now Peter would be in a bad mood, and their last night in Hawaii didn't sound very promising with a sullen boyfriend.

"We lost," Alice said.

"I don't care." Haley pushed her hair behind her ears. "I couldn't wait for the game to be over."

"Aren't you worried Scott will be mad about losing?"

“He doesn’t look too ruffled.” Haley waved and smiled at him.

Scott flashed her friend a grin that indeed said he didn’t care much about the final score. Haley and Scott had officially become an item. Yesterday, the only game-free day in their trip, the four of them had spent the entire day at the beach. And the new couple had been inseparable; they hadn’t stopped kissing for more than two minutes. Last night, finally, they’d managed to swap rooms without incident. After a night with Scott, Haley had come to breakfast with a smile so bright it had told Alice all she needed to know.

Alice watched as the team gathered their gear and disappeared into the locker room. There were only two people with expressions darker than Peter’s: Jack’s and, well, David’s. The older Williams brother didn’t seem to have taken Haley and Scott getting together lightly. But he hadn’t pulled another stunt since their first night on the island. Instead, he opted to keep a haughty, detached attitude. And Jack… well, he’d been a jerk for the whole trip. Alice couldn’t pinpoint exactly what bothered her so much about his behavior. It wasn’t just that he’d done his best to avoid her; he acted as if he couldn’t stand to look at her. It was clear he was annoyed she’d come on this trip. Why? Had she stolen his preferred wingman? The thought made her bristle.

“Let’s go,” Haley said. “I can’t believe we’re flying home tomorrow. I don’t want to lose one minute we have left.”

Alice followed her friend out of their seats toward the stadium exit. “Yeah, sure.”

Her mind was on a completely different page. She couldn't wait to be home and craved the comforting view of the snow-covered campus and the chill, time-of-the-year-appropriate temperatures. But most of all, she wanted to be alone. No Peter and no Jack. This whole trip seemed like a huge mistake and a total waste of money at this point. She would have counted Haley's new romance a success, except that it was with the guy her other best friend had a crush on. All in all, a complete fiasco.

Madison would be devastated. Haley's happiness was so obvious and in-your-face it left no room for interpretation. Alice could only hope Madison's infatuation for Scott wasn't as deep as she suspected. Because from the way he and Haley kept looking at each other, Haley's strong feelings were reciprocated.

What a mess. What a complete, utter mess.

***

Alice's worries proved true the following night. When they arrived back home at the apartment, Alice noticed Madison staring at Haley's ecstatic smile with a look of pure dread.

"Merry Christmas," Madison said. "Only a day late."

Haley twirled around the living room, blind to Madison's discomfort. "It's been a very, very merry Christmas!"

"Yeah?" Madison wringed her fingers, steadying herself for the bad news. "So the trip went well?"

"Better!" Haley spread her arms wide and kept spinning. "I left single and came back in love," she announced in a singsong voice.

Madison paled. "With who?"

"The best guy in the world: Scott Williams!"

Haley was too excited to notice how Madison drained completely of color and had to lean against the couch for support.

"I can't wait for you to meet him," Haley continued. "He's so great."

"Actually, I-I do k-know him," Madison spluttered.

"You do?" Haley was genuinely surprised. "How come?"

"English concentration, remember?" Madison's voice carried a ring of accusation. "I told you when we went to see that basketball game."

"How am I supposed to remember from so long ago?" Haley dismissed her. "Anyway, he's Superman when it comes to courses."

"What do you mean?" Alice purposely injected herself into the conversation to give Madison a minute to recover.

"He's taking all these pre-med courses on top of his main English concentration, on top of basketball. He's superhuman."

Alice checked she'd heard right. "So he wants to go to Med School, but he's majoring in English?"

"Yeah, says it's his passion." Haley shrugged. "You should ask the other poet in the room." She jerked her chin toward Madison. "I'll never understand why people spend so much time reading all that stuff dead people wrote."

"Just because the only thing you enjoy reading is lines of code," Madison snapped, "doesn't mean all other people shouldn't care about literature."

Haley lifted her hands in surrender. "No one's touching your precious Shakespeare, don't worry. Wow, I can't say a thing about books without you getting all touchy. Hands-off lit, I promise."

Oh, Haley. She had no clue Madison's attitude had nothing to do with literature. It was more of a hands-off-*Scott* issue.

Madison blanked out Haley and turned to Alice. "Did you have a good time too?"

"Yeah, but I got so mad at—"

"I'm hopping in the shower and then straight to bed," Haley interrupted. "I'm beat."

"Good night," Alice said.

"Night." Haley disappeared inside the bathroom.

"You were saying?" Madison asked.

Now that Haley was out of hearing range, Alice asked, "Are you okay?"

"I'd rather not talk about it," Madison said, close to tears. She was visibly struggling to choke back a lump in her throat. "Can you distract me with your own boy problems?"

"Are you sure?"

"Yeah." Madison nodded. "We'll talk about it, but not now. Can I keep Blue tonight?"

"Sure." Alice walked into her room to pick up the bunny. She brought him into Madison's room and sat on the bed next to her. "Here, bunny joy for you."

"Thanks." Madison took Blue and placed him on her lap. He squealed at being handled, then relaxed when Madison started stroking him. "So was it Jack or Peter who pissed you off?"

"Jack, for the most part."

Alice started telling her friend about Hawaii, focusing on how Jack had ignored her, and leaving out Haley and Scott's romance. If Madison wasn't ready to discuss her feelings for Scott, giving her a break was the least Alice could do. And she had enough Jack-complaints to keep talking all night long.

Twenty-four

Alice

The weekend before the start of Spring Term, Alice received a text from Georgiana. Her mentor was back from Paris and she wanted to meet up.

Alice popped her head inside Madison's room. "Hey. You busy?"

Her roommate was lying on her made-up bed, enthralled by some nineteenth-century literary tome.

Madison raised her bespectacled face. "Huh?" Her expression was one of not-so-veiled annoyance that she usually gave when someone interrupted her reading.

"Georgiana is back from Paris," Alice said. "I'm meeting her for coffee."

Madison lowered the book to her knees. "So she didn't stay in Paris? *Pity.*"

"Eh..." Alice could not understand how two people—cousins—she liked so much could despise each other. At least, she knew Madison didn't like Georgiana—she wasn't sure if it went the other way around, too. "I take it you wouldn't want to join us?"

"I'd rather stick a fork in each of my eyes."

"How would you read, then?"

"Audiobooks."

Alice walked into the room and sat on the only chair available next to Madison's desk. "I honestly can't understand why you don't get along with her."

Madison snorted. "And I *honestly* don't understand how you can be so blind to the fact that my dear cousin is a stone-cold bitch!"

"She's always been kind to me."

"You must be part of an elite group of chosen ones." Madison drummed her fingers on the hard cover of her book. "As for the rest of us, we only get to see her Queen Bee side. Everything has to be about her and never anyone else."

"But did she ever do something bad to you?" Alice asked.

"You mean like stealing my boyfriend?"

Now, that explained a lot of things. "She did that? I didn't know."

"Well, it's not like she's going to tell you or even admit it. If you asked her, she'd tell you he wasn't really my boyfriend. That the relationship was all in my head since I had a childish infatuation. And, anyway, she couldn't help it if he loved her and not me."

Alice did not recall Madison ever being with someone in a long-term relationship. "When was this?"

"High school. I was a freshman, and she couldn't stand me dating a senior. She didn't even like him; she did it just to spite me." Madison's features contracted in anger. "She made freshman year a nightmare for me; the day she graduated was the best day of my life."

"Sounds like a long time ago," Alice said. "Couldn't you give your cousin a second chance?"

Madison huffed. "Listen, Alice. I know she's your friend and I'm glad she's nice to you. But we're like oil and water; we don't mix. I already have to spend spring break trapped on a tiny island with her; I want to avoid any unnecessary suffering."

"Okay, okay. I get the message." Alice lifted her hands in surrender. "Where are you going for spring break?"

"Martha's Vineyard. It's my other cousin's—Vicky, the nice one—wedding, and she made it a one-week event in the middle of March on an island you shouldn't touch until late May or June. But never mind, she's the one cousin I love."

Alice chuckled. "Your family is complicated."

"You tell me."

"I gotta go now."

"Have a good time with Maleficent." Madison waved, then stuck her nose back in her book.

Alice stopped at the door. "Are you sure you'll be all right? Is Haley out, too?"

Madison lifted her gaze again. "She's at Scott's, I think. And Alice, I'm not suicidal. You can leave me alone for an afternoon, I promise."

Madison was trying to appear strong, but Alice could tell she was in a lot of pain.

"Okay. I'll see you later," Alice said. She still felt responsible for what had happened between Haley and Scott. She'd made one of her best friends the happiest person in the world, and the other miserable.

Madison smiled, then made a point of staring intently at her book. The this-conversation-is-over message all too clear.

Alice walked out of the room, guilt comfortably nestled on her shoulders.

***

Georgiana was waiting for Alice at the Starbucks on Broadway. She'd already ordered two venti cappuccinos and was seated at a round table in the corner near the wall-wide window.

"Hey," Alice greeted.

Georgiana's eyes widened. "Whoa, it's you." She stood up to hug her. "Alice Brown! For a moment, I didn't recognize you. This new hairstyle is amazing. When did you dye it?"

"A while ago. I needed a change." Alice shrugged. She had forgotten the last time she'd seen Georgiana, she'd been a blonde. "You look amazing, too."

They both sat down. The weather was freezing, and Alice gladly wrapped her hands around the warm coffee cup.

"I can't be that amazing." Georgiana pinched herself on a cheek. "I'm still super jet-lagged. We landed only last night."

Georgiana loved false modesty. Right now, she had the look of a porcelain doll: perfect skin, perfect hair, no bags under her eyes, and no signs of tiredness on her face.

Alice ignored the bait for compliments. "How was Paris?"

"The usual." Georgiana waved a hand casually. "Cultured, so European and romantic."

"Is everything good with Tyler then?"

Georgiana's boyfriend hadn't exactly been eager to move across the globe for a semester. Georgiana had pulled some serious strings in the exchange program so that she and Tyler could go to Paris. All to keep him away from his best friend Rose—now Ethan's girlfriend.

Georgiana tilted her head to one side, then the other. "Yes and no."

"What do you mean?"

"I think there's still something going on between him and Rose." Georgiana paused and stared at her with big eyes. "By the way, I was so sorry to hear my idiot of a brother dumped you for her. You're so many leagues above her, it doesn't make sense."

Alice waved her off. "Ah, it was a long time ago. I'm over it."

"Dating anyone new?"

Alice took a sip of coffee before saying, "Yeah." She gave Georgiana the highlights of her relationship with Peter. They did the conventional round of Facebook stalking on their phones before Alice brought the conversation back to Georgiana's love life. "So, Tyler and Rose; why are you still suspicious?"

"Have you ever had a male best friend?" Georgiana asked.

Jack. "Yeah, why?"

"If you didn't have an interest in him that went beyond friendship, would you stop talking to him if he moved to Paris for a semester with his girlfriend?"

The thought of Jack in Paris for a semester with an imaginary girlfriend chilled Alice to the bone. She hadn't told Georgiana about her feelings for Jack. The only two people Alice had trusted with the knowledge were Madison and Haley.

So Alice decided to give Georgiana a neutral answer. "If I didn't have feelings for the guy, no. I'd be happy for him to have this opportunity. Why? Rose and Tyler stopped talking because he moved to Paris with you?"

"More or less. In the weeks before we left, Rose went AWOL." Georgiana's eyes sparked maliciously. "I know they didn't talk much, if at all, while we were there, and she moved out of his house a month after we left."

"Wasn't she there only temporarily, to begin with?"

"In theory, yes." Georgiana leaned forward, lowering her voice. "But before Paris, she wasn't even looking for a place. I kept arguing with Tyler about it. Then she gets the house all to herself and moves out in a blink. Why the rush?"

"Is she still dating your brother?"

"Unfortunately, yes," Georgiana admitted. "She couldn't get her claws in my boyfriend, so she stuck them in my brother instead."

"But if she's dating Ethan, she won't be after Tyler anymore," Alice pointed out.

"I don't know." Georgiana leaned back in her chair, unconvinced. "With a girl like that, she might want to have her cake and eat it, too."

"So, what are you going to do?"

"Nothing for now. I'll see how things evolve." Georgiana pursed her lips, determined, before adding, "But I'm not leaving Tyler to her if it's the last thing I do."

Alice secretly thanked the sky above that Jack had never had a girlfriend this resolute. Why was she thinking about Jack, anyway? Her boyfriend was Peter. *P. E. T. E. R.*

"I'll ask Tyler to come to my sister's wedding with me," Georgiana continued. "If he says yes, it'll show how committed he is."

"Ah, yes. On Martha's Vineyard, right? Madison told me about it."

Georgiana winced. "Sometimes I forget my cousin is your roommate. That must be a pain; she's so boring." Georgiana made a gesture as if she was swatting away an annoying fly.

Maybe Madison's prejudices weren't all inside her head.

"We get along well," Alice said noncommittally. "Will Ethan bring Rose to the wedding?"

"He's stupid enough to ask her, I'm afraid." Her friend sighed. "Call it a happy reunion."

"Well, at least you'll be able to study how she and Tyler interact."

"Yeah, that's the only silver lining. What about you? Any fun plans for spring break?"

"Not yet." Alice shrugged. "Something fun with Peter, hopefully. The basketball season will end in early March, so he'll have more free time."

Another trip with Peter. Alice wasn't that eager but tried to be optimistic. A basketball-free, Jack-free trip, had real potential.

Twenty-five

Haley

Haley was about to press Scott's doorbell when the door opened and she found herself staring into David's blue eyes.

His face switched from surprised to coy in a heartbeat. "Hello, Sunshine," he greeted her.

"I'm here to see your brother," Haley said.

"State the obvious, won't you?"

"Is he home?"

David shook his head. "Nope."

"We were supposed to meet here at 3," Haley explained. "Can I wait for him inside?"

David smiled that infuriating smirk of his and opened the door wide, presenting the inside of the house to her. "Come on in."

"So you guys live together?" she asked as she took off her scarf and coat and draped them on the back of an armchair in the living room.

"Unfortunately. My parents refuse to pay for separate accommodations." David closed the door and walked back inside the apartment. "So yeah, I'm stuck with my virtuous younger brother as a roommate."

"Why do you always have to do that?"

"Do what?" David raised his eyebrows.

"Speak as if you mean the exact opposite of what you say."

"Oh, that." David chuckled. "It's called sarcasm."

"I get it; you have it in for Scott. But can't you get over it?"

David's eyes blazed. "Get over what, exactly?"

Haley lowered her gaze, unable to meet his eyes, as she whispered, "He told me about Brigitte."

"Oh, yeah?" David gritted his teeth. "And what exactly did he tell you?"

"He told me you both liked her in high school, and that she chose him."

"That's rich!" David's nostrils flared wide as he stared at the ceiling.

"What's rich?"

"That little tale my brother fed you."

"You're doing it again: hinting at some mysterious, hidden truth and never saying what's on your mind!"

"I hate to break it to you, Princess, but with me what you see is what you get." He pointed down at himself. "I don't pretend to be good when I'm not. And I don't pretend to be a righteous son-of-a-bitch when I'm not."

"Again, you don't say it, but you're implying Scott does pretend to be something he's not."

David shrugged, apparently calm again. "Your words, not mine."

"And what would he be lying about?"

"Ah, see." David's smirk was bitter this time. "To lie outright wouldn't be Scott's style. He prefers to omit. That Brigitte story, he conveniently left half of it out so he wouldn't look bad."

"What did he leave out?" Haley asked.

"I'm sorry, I can only give sarcastic, half-true answers… So why don't you ask your *boyfriend*."

David put so much hatred into the word "boyfriend" that Haley recoiled. She wondered how it was possible for the two of them to live together without either of them having killed the other yet.

She refused to let David provoke her. "You're just trying to screw with my head."

"Tell yourself whatever you need to sleep at night."

"I don't need to tell myself anything," Haley snapped.

"Good for you." David walked back to the door and opened it. "I trust I can leave you here without you scavenging the place, yeah?"

Haley sat on the couch and crossed her arms over her chest, glaring at him. "I'll wait right here."

"Perfect. Don't wait up for me." He slammed the front door as he left.

Haley wanted to scream. She shouldn't let him get to her. How did he manage to get under her skin so easily and so quickly?

To distract herself, Haley studied the room, taking in details of the house. Definitely a guy's apartment. The couch was brown leather with plastic compartments to hold glasses or beer cans. She swiped a finger over the rim of one. Everything else screamed model-house as if this were the apartment they used to show for visits; it was all plain furniture. The only personalizing touches were basketball-themed items casually propped here and there around the house, and a huge flat-screen TV.

She wondered what the bedrooms looked like. Could she get away with taking a quick peek? But what if Scott came home and found her snooping in David's room? She'd be so busted. Haley checked her watch; he was supposed to have been here fifteen minutes ago. It couldn't be much longer until he arrived.

As if on cue, Haley heard a key turn in the keyhole and the door opening. She got to her feet.

"Haley, you're here," Scott said. He seemed surprised to find her inside. "I'm so sorry I was late, I was reading and lost track of time."

"It doesn't matter. David let me in."

Scott's face immediately darkened. "I'm surprised he was here. He's usually never at home."

"He was headed out," Haley said. "Said not to wait up for him."

Scott looked wary. "Is that all he said?"

Haley considered how to answer. She didn't want David to stir up problems between her and Scott, which had clearly been his intention, but she was too curious about Brigitte to let it go.

"We had a bit of an argument actually," Haley said, hugging herself.

Scott took three quick strides across the room and braced his hands on her shoulders "Did he do something to you?" he asked, looking at her with a worried expression.

"No." Haley shrugged free and sat down. "He didn't do anything. He said things."

"What things?" Scott sat next to her.

"He said you haven't told me the whole truth about Brigitte."

Scott massaged his temples with his fingers. "What else?"

"Nothing. That's all he said."

"All right." Scott sighed and faced Haley. "David has this idea in his head of how things happened that's not true."

"Okay…"

"Listen, you shouldn't let him get to you like this."

"I know. But I can sense you're not telling me something, and it feels like David's trying to use that against us." Haley was tired of Scott's instant semi-muteness whenever David or Brigitte were mentioned. "So what's the truth?"

"I don't like to talk about that period of my life."

"I get that," Haley said. "But if you don't tell me, I'll never know which one of you I should believe."

Scott scoffed. "See? You're already starting to doubt me. That's exactly what he wants."

"And also why we're talking about it," Haley insisted. "Listen, you can't tell me David's got the wrong idea without telling me why or about what."

Scott sighed. "All right. I'll tell you everything." He leaned his back against the couch and spoke, looking at the ceiling. "Brigitte was my first. The first girl I loved, my first everything. She was beautiful, playful, and she had this impossible-to-resist French accent that would make any guy lose his mind."

"Okay, you don't need to be that specific," Haley joked.

"Sorry." Scott smirked. "Anyway, from the first day she set foot in our school, David had his eyes on her, and so did I. But I was shy and inexperienced and he was not. They started dating almost immediately."

"Then what happened?"

"She was my age, a year younger than David, so we had a lot of classes together and we started talking. She had a compelling personality. It was impossible not to fall for her, especially for a shy guy like me. At one point she started complaining about my brother, said their relationship wasn't working. Finally, one day she told me they'd broken up."

"Was it true?"

"I believed her. I wanted to believe her so badly."

"So, she was lying?" This Brigitte character wasn't growing on Haley. The opposite, in fact.

"Yeah."

"And you couldn't tell?"

"No." Scott shifted position and finally met her gaze. "I never saw her with David anymore, and I had no reason to assume she was lying."

"So you two… what?"

"Exactly what you think. We were together while she was still seeing David."

"I don't understand. What did David do?"

"He didn't know." Scott shook his head. "Brigitte told me we had to keep our relationship a secret. She explained it by saying she didn't want to hurt David's feelings, that it was too soon for us to date openly… blah, blah, blah. I was young and in love, gullible enough to go along with it if it meant I could be with her."

"It didn't last, I take it."

"No. David found us together." The shadow of a bad memory crossed Scott's face. "We got into this huge fight, and then we told Brigitte she had to choose."

"And she chose you," Haley finished for him.

"And that, David will never forgive."

"So you stayed with her, even after she lied to you like that?"

"As I said, I was young, stupid, and in love."

Haley put the last pieces together. "David doesn't believe you didn't know."

"No, I don't think he does. And the fact that I kept going out with Brigitte afterward was proof enough for him."

Haley honestly could not blame him. "How long were you with her?"

"At the end of the year she moved back to France, and David moved on to college. This wound between us has been festering ever since."

"Well, at least now it makes sense why he behaves like that." Haley's head was spinning with all this new information. "Haven't you tried to explain to him how it really happened? It seems to me this Brigitte person was pretty awful."

"In hindsight, she was," Scott agreed. "And I've tried to talk with my brother a million times, but he won't listen."

"I'm sorry for dredging all of this up." Haley squeezed Scott's upper arm. "But I needed to know."

"And I'm glad I told you the whole story."

"Come here," Haley said.

She opened her arms to hold Scott to her chest as she leaned back on the couch. Haley stared at the ceiling, enjoying Scott's weight on her. But as she stroked his hair, she couldn't help but feel sorry for David.

Twenty-six

Alice

"You guys," Madison called, strolling across the living room with a huge suitcase in tow. "I'm off. Wish me luck for the worst spring break ever!"

Alice interrupted her own packing and emerged from her room to say goodbye. "Oh, come on," she said. "It won't be that bad!"

"A week stuck on a tiny island with my entire family?" Madison rolled her eyes. "Yeah, it will."

Haley joined them. "If it's any consolation," she said, "I've been conscripted by my parents as well after skipping Christmas." Haley hugged Madison and then eyed Alice sideways. "She's the only one who's going to have a good time."

"I'm sure you guys will have just as much fun," Alice said defensively.

"Yeah." Madison snorted. She lifted one hand and lowered the other as if weighing options on an imaginary scale. "Boring family wedding on freezing Martha's Vineyard." She reversed the height of her hands. "Or amazing trip with hot boyfriend in sunny Miami. Mmm… you're right. It's hard to call!"

"Oh, shut up." Alice shoved her away playfully.

"At least you're going somewhere, and weddings are fun," Haley protested. "I'm just going to be confined at home for a week."

"Trust me," Madison exhaled. "If you'd met even half my family, a week in *your* house would look like paradise."

"You could always meet cute wedding guests," Alice offered.

"I don't know." Madison frowned. "All Vicky's friends are lawyers."

"What's wrong with lawyers?" Haley asked.

"Seriously?" Madison said, incredulous.

"I mean," Haley continued, "aren't you supposed to become one as well?"

A shadow crossed Madison's face. "We'll see." She sighed. "I'd better go or I'll be late. See you guys."

They did a three-way hug, and then Madison left.

"Are you leaving today as well?" Haley asked, once Madison was gone.

"No, Peter is picking me up tomorrow," Alice replied. "You?"

Haley checked her watch. "I have an Uber booked in half an hour. I'd better go finish packing!"

A short while later, Haley called out again to announce she was leaving. Alice hugged her friend goodbye, walked her to the door, and turned around to an empty apartment. She wrapped her arms around her chest, hugging herself. It felt weird to be here alone. Should she call Peter and ask him to spend the night? It would make sense as they had to leave for the airport early the next morning. As sensible as it was, the idea did not appeal to Alice. She'd rather be alone.

You'd rather be with Jack, a treacherous voice echoed in her head.

"No, I wouldn't," Alice said aloud.

Liar.

Alice sank on the couch. Okay, she was lying. The thought of being away from Jack for a week was depressing. Even if they didn't spend as much time together as they'd used to. She still saw him in class every day, and most weekends at games. Even at Christmas, seeing him in small, annoying doses had been better than not seeing him at all.

Alice threw a pillow across the living room and let out a frustrated scream. "Why can't I just forget him?" she asked the ceiling.

No reply came.

***

After an uneventful trip, Alice and Peter landed at Miami Airport mid-morning and took a cab to Peter's house. His parents owned a condo apartment in South Beach, and they'd agreed to let him use it during spring break. Alice couldn't have afforded to pay for a hotel on top of the flight, not after Christmas's detour to Hawaii.

Peter's house was a glassy, two-story apartment. Wall-wide windows and white, minimalist furniture were the main theme. They stopped there only long enough to drop their luggage and change for the beach, and then they were off. When they reached the sandy shore, Peter rented two lounge chairs from a booth and collapsed on his as soon as it was delivered. He was asleep in a matter of minutes.

Alice coated herself in sunscreen and tried to relax by reading a book. Too soon, her skin heated up. The wind wasn't cool enough to counter the smothering midday heat. Half-bored by the book and definitely too hot, Alice decided to take a walk along the beach to distract herself. She dipped her toes in the ocean, then returned to the loungers and picked her book back up. When she got bored again, it was back to the water. She repeated this cycle several times, and Peter slept through all of it.

By the time he finally stirred, Alice was itching to make plans for all the things they should go see and the nice restaurants they could visit. It was her first visit to Florida, and Alice couldn't wait to explore a new city and, possibly, the Everglades and Key West. She'd also heard the Cuban food was great here. Maybe Peter knew a good place to have an authentic taste. He said he didn't.

"Do you think we can drive to Key West?" Alice asked next.

Peter groaned. "Yo, it's a four-hour drive."

"So?" Alice stiffened on her chair. "We have a week."

"There's not that much to see, plus I'd like to relax. Spend the week with my friends here in Miami. It's really not worth it to waste a day to drive down there."

Alice bit her lower lip in frustration, trying to suppress the angry retort that wanted so badly to come out. She really wanted to see the Keys, but this was Peter's vacation too. If he wanted to stay in Miami…

"How about the Everglades? I've always wanted to ride one of those crazy boats with the giant fan in the back." *They look so exciting in the movies.*

Peter shaded his eyes with one hand to look at her. "A hovercraft?"

"Yeah, that's it. Can we go on one?"

"Sure." He tilted his head back toward the sun, eyes closed. "A friend of mine has one he uses to fish. We can get a ride with him."

At least Peter had finally agreed to do *something* fun.

"You want to take a walk down Ocean Drive with me?" she asked.

"Babe, relax." He threw her a reproachful, one-eyed stare. "Can't you just enjoy the sun? I'm chilling here."

Alice fought hard to keep her temper in check. "Is 'chilling' all you plan to do while we're here?"

"Don't worry babe, I have it all planned out. We're having a party at the house tonight."

"A party?"

Shouldn't he at least have asked her if she wanted to have a party on their first night in Miami? Alice was anticipating a quiet, romantic dinner, not a house party.

"Yeah, I've invited a few friends over," Peter said casually.

"Should we buy something? The house is a bit understocked."

"Nah, there's a liquor store a block from the house."

"What about food?"

"They have Doritos and stuff at the store."

This didn't sound like the kind of party Alice would enjoy. She had a sinking feeling this trip would not end well, possibly even worse than Hawaii. "I'm going for a walk," she snapped. "See you back at the house."

She stood up from the lounging chair to go have a look around Ocean Drive by herself. Dread filled her as she thought about the party they were supposed to host in a few hours.

***

At three in the morning, Alice had had enough. What were supposed to be a "few" friends had turned out to be half of Miami. *The worse half.* Peter's friends were either too drunk to talk, or too obnoxious if they could still manage to string two words together. She felt like a fish out of water. There wasn't a single person in the house she wanted to meet or try to chat up. Her head was throbbing, thanks to the loud music drilling a steady boom-boom-boom in her brain. She'd even considered calling the cops on her boyfriend just so she could finally go to bed. Enough was enough.

Alice walked toward Peter and poked him in the shoulder. "I'm going to bed," she said.

"Oh, baby. Already?" He slurred his words. "But the fun is just starting."

"I've had enough *fun* for tonight," Alice hissed, sure that Peter would miss the sarcasm in her voice.

"All right." Peter ruffled her hair, and it took all her self-control not to swat his hand away. "Go to the upstairs bedroom, the guys know it's off-limits."

The fact that the downstairs bedrooms were clearly *not* off-limits made Alice's stomach heave.

"Good night," she said, her tone glacial.

Peter grabbed her by the waist. "Night," he said, then tried to kiss her on the lips. As he drew closer, a whiff of his breath—a disgusting mix of beer and cheap vodka—smacked Alice. Repulsed, she turned her face and Peter's lips landed on her left cheek.

Alice wiggled away and almost ran across the room and up the stairs to the safety of the upper floor. She changed into her PJs and locked herself in the master bedroom. She didn't care that Peter might not be able to come in later in the night. There was no chance in hell she would sleep with him tonight—literally or otherwise. She hoped this horrific first day had been a one-off and that Peter would get all this frat-boy partying out of his system for good. Because if this was how he planned to spend the whole week, Alice could see herself renting a car and driving to the Keys alone.

Twenty-seven
Jack

Jack walked out of the arrival gate of Indianapolis airport, searching the crowd with his eyes. He spotted Felicity at once; she was holding an iPad with "Mr. Sullivan" handwritten on the screen. He looked at her with fondness. His ex-girlfriend and oldest friend wasn't classically beautiful—short, with squashed features, and a little on the chubby side—but her impeccable grooming and bubbly personality made her attractive. Jack was home because he hadn't seen his parents at Christmas. As for Felicity, Jack suspected she'd come home to spend spring break with him.

Felicity insisted on denying it, but Jack was sure she still loved him. No matter that their relationship had ended more than three years ago. Her feelings for him had always been fiercer and, apparently, longer lived.

She saw him and her entire face brightened. Jack's heart sank a little. Every time he saw her, he couldn't help remembering the day he'd broken her heart. The way she'd cried and screamed how much she hated him. The way his chest had exploded with guilt at causing her so much pain. And the solitude that had followed that summer after he'd lost his best friend.

"Jack!" Felicity waved a hand above her head and ran toward him.

She barreled into him and he scooped her up in his arms, lifting her feet off the ground.

"It's so good to see you," she said.

"You too, Felix." Jack ruffled her blonde hair fondly.

"I can't believe you're here. It's been forever!"

"When did you land?" Jack asked.

"Early this morning. I caught a late flight last night."

Felicity was studying at Berkley. After their breakup senior year, before they'd somehow patched their relationship, Felix had gone to school as far away from Jack as she could.

"But I still look fresher than you," Felix added, eyeing him sideways as they walked toward her car. "What's up with you, Sullivan?"

Jack grimaced. What was up with him was that Ice had decided to spend spring break in Miami with Peter. But Jack wasn't comfortable discussing his feelings for another woman with Felicity. Especially not in person when he could witness all the tiny giveaways of her discomfort in the creases on her face.

Jack shrugged. "Nothing. I'm just tired."

Felicity didn't look convinced, but she didn't press him. They reached her car and spent the rest of the journey in silence, with Felicity driving and Jack staring out the window. She dropped him at his parents' house, and they agreed to meet up later for a beer.

***

Jack was in his parents' garden in front of the rock fire pit. The sun had set a while ago and Jack had lit the gas fire to keep warm. He was staring at the flames, sipping beer from the bottle, when Felicity walked out from the house and sat on the chair next to him.

"You're worrying your mother, you know," she said by way of greeting.

"My mom?" Jack raised his brows, still looking at the fire. "Why?"

Felicity wrapped herself in one of the outside blankets and dragged her chair closer to the fire. "Maybe because you're sitting outside when it's fifty degrees?"

"I have the fire to keep warm."

"Or maybe it's that you're drinking beer alone, looking sadder than when your Teenage Mutant Ninja Turtles went missing."

Despite his bad mood, Jack's lips twitched. Losing his favorite action figures had been the biggest tragedy of his childhood. He turned to face Felix. "I'm not alone. You're here."

"Open this." She handed him a beer bottle. "Your dad said you kidnapped the bottle opener."

Jack took the bottle, cracked the cap open, and gave it back.

Felicity took a sip and sighed. "Is this brooding still about that girl at Harvard?"

No point in lying. Jack turned toward the fire again and nodded.

Felicity scoffed. "Have you talked to her?"

Jack shook his head.

"Jack Sullivan, look at me."

He did.

"Tell her how you feel."

"What's the point? Ice has a boyfriend."

"That's because she doesn't have all the information."

"You haven't seen them together." A flash of Alice and Peter making out on the bed in Hawaii appeared in his mind's eye. "She's in love with Peter."

"Or maybe," Felicity said in her I'm-spelling-it-out-for-you voice, "she's in love with you and is using this Peter guy as a distraction because she thinks she can't have you."

Jack glared at his friend. "You don't even know her."

"Believe me." Felicity turned red. "It's very difficult to get over you."

Guilt gnawed at Jack again. It was clear Felicity was projecting herself onto Alice. But Ice wasn't Felicity, and she wasn't in love with him. "Listen, Felix. She's been with Peter for months. They're in Miami now on a romantic getaway. Trust me, she's not in love with me."

"How do you know? Have you ever asked her?"

"Ice wouldn't be dating Peter if she loved me."

"Again, she doesn't have all the info."

"What difference would it make?"

"Jack, can't you see?" Felix sounded exasperated. "She tried to kiss you, and you said you wanted to be her friend. She has no idea how you feel."

"But why date Peter?"

"To make you jealous?"

"Even if she did at the beginning, now they've been together too long."

"Okay, maybe Alice likes this Peter dude, but do you know for sure if she's in love with him?"

"No."

"So stop being such a crybaby and talk to her. What are you waiting for?"

"Peter graduates in a few months."

"So your plan is to wait for him to be out of the picture?"

Jack shrugged. "Maybe." Actually, that was exactly his plan. Peter would get a contract with some big team and move away from Boston. And, yes, Jack imagined himself as the shoulder for Alice to cry on.

"That's a losing strategy."

"Why?"

"If you want the girl, go get her. Don't wait for her to fall into your lap. *Fight.*"

"And what if I lose?"

"You wouldn't be worse off than now. You've got nothing to lose and everything to gain from talking to her."

Jack's eyes reflected the fire's dancing flames. Could Felicity be right? Had he wasted all these months brooding instead of fighting for what he wanted? He had to at least try. Jack pursed his lips in a determined pout. Peter had had it easy so far, but that was about to change.

Twenty-eight
Alice

Alice didn't drive alone to the Keys. She should have, but instead, she endured a full week of Peter's crazy partying, his sleeping in late, and his constant "chilling." She saw what she could of Miami in the mornings when Peter was so wasted he wouldn't even get out of bed to go to the beach. He had made her hate Miami and everyone from Florida. And the worst part was that he hadn't even noticed something was terribly wrong. By the time they returned to Boston and parted ways, Alice was amazed that she'd managed to keep her cool the entire trip.

Back at her apartment, she finally let out all her frustration as she and her roommates discussed their respective trips from hell whilst doing their nails in the living room.

"You guys," Alice said, scowling at Madison and Haley, "I'm telling you, he was too wasted to help me clean up."

"So you had to clean his parents' place by yourself?" Haley demanded incredulously. She paused in applying her black polish to stare up at Alice, her brush hanging in mid-air. "Why? I mean, what do *you* care if he left the place trashed?"

"I was a guest in his parents' house, too." Alice winced at the memory of the dirty apartment after a week of non-stop partying. "I couldn't leave their house trashed."

"You should've let him handle it," Haley insisted.

"I agree," Madison said.

"Believe me, girls," Alice insisted, "if you'd seen the place, you would've been just as compelled to clean it up." She lifted her shoulders in a gesture of impotence.

"So you were in Florida for a week and all you did was babysit a drunk Peter?" Haley asked.

Alice nodded in misery. "That's depressingly accurate. It's like he had to make up for the entire basketball season and compress five months of lost parties into a single week."

"No romantic drive to the Keys?" Madison asked.

"Nope."

"But you did do something romantic in Miami?" Madison insisted.

"No, not even one dinner." Alice wished she didn't sound so bitter. "I survived on Doritos and hot dogs for a week."

"No Everglades?" Haley offered.

"Too 'touristy' according to Peter, but I managed to have him arrange a ride on a hovercraft."

"That sounds exciting," Haley said. "See, you and Peter did something fun."

"Oh, yeah. His friend drove me around the swamp while Peter drank beer with some other friends back at this guy's fishing shack. Great fun."

"At least your tan looks awesome," Madison said. "Better than family duty for a week."

"Yeah," Haley agreed. "You had the best spring break among the three of us, by far, so please stop complaining about partying too much."

"I would've rather spent the week being cuddled by my mom," Alice said. "I swear."

Haley glowered at her, so Alice turned to Madison, changing the subject. "How was the wedding?"

Madison stopped blowing air on her shiny coral nails and said, "Vicky was a beautiful bride."

"Any cute boys?" Haley asked.

"Not one!" Madison sighed.

Alice stared down at her blue nails, not liking the result. "How was Georgiana?" she asked, as she began to remove the polish with a cotton disk.

Madison winced; a common reaction when anyone mentioned Georgiana in her presence. "Her usual nasty self."

Alice was curious about the whole Georgiana-Rose-Tyler love triangle. "Was Tyler there?"

"Yep. Rose and Ethan were there, too."

Correction: quadrangle including Ethan in the picture.

Alice finished removing the last specks of blue and started applying a nude miracle gel to her pinkie. "So, did you pick up any weird vibes?" she asked.

"Why?" Haley asked, puzzled. "What's going on?"

Madison launched into an explanation. "My cousin, Georgiana, suspects her boyfriend, Tyler, has a thing for his best friend, Rose. Or, equally bad, that Rose is trying to steal him from her. Only Rose was at the wedding as Ethan's date. He's my other cousin, Georgiana's older brother, and Alice's ex."

Haley raised both her eyebrows. "Come again?"

"I said my cousin Georgiana—"

"Yeah, I got all that the first time," Haley interrupted. "It just sounded too soap-opera to be real."

"So, is it?" Alice asked. "Did any of it seem real to you?"

"Well." Madison thought for a second. "Rose and Tyler definitely seemed awkward around each other. And Georgiana stared daggers at her for the entire week. Moved the target from its usual spot behind my back, actually. But from the way Rose and Ethan were staring at each other the entire time… Sorry, Alice…"

"Don't worry." Alice shook her head. "He's ancient history."

"They seemed smitten," Madison concluded. "So, no, I don't think Rose is trying to steal Tyler."

"What about your cousin and this… Tyler?" Haley asked.

"That, I'm not sure about. I caught him looking at Rose with a brooding expression one too many times."

"So Georgiana wasn't entirely wrong," Alice mused. "There could've been something between Rose and Tyler at one point."

"If there ever was, Rose is over it," Madison said, confident. "And I hope for his sake, Tyler will be over my *sweet* cousin soon, too."

"Oh, come on," Alice chided.

Madison shrugged. "He didn't seem much into her, anyway." She turned to Haley. "What about you? How was your break?"

"In one word, *boring*," Haley replied. "But I didn't have to cook, and my mom did my laundry! She ironed my pajamas. Ironed PJs, can you guys believe it?"

Alice and Madison chuckled.

"I'm being serious," Haley insisted. "It was way too cold to do anything remotely fun—"

"Not as cold as Martha's Vineyard," Madison interrupted. "I promise."

"Still cold enough to spoil every outdoor activity. Plus, none of my friends was there. They all came back for Thanksgiving or Christmas, but definitely not spring break. It was a desert town."

"What did you do all day?" Alice asked.

"Honestly? I coded, I slept, and I ate my mom's food. I win the price for lamest spring break ever."

"Yeah." Alice smiled playfully. "I'm afraid you do."

"Anyway," Haley continued, "next weekend I'll come up with something amazing to cure our back-to-school blues." She paused to look them in the eyes. "And that, you guys, is a promise."

***

"Roomies!" Haley sang as she burst into the living room the next Saturday. "What do you say we all go out together tonight?"

"Define 'we,'" Madison said.

"Define 'out,'" Alice echoed.

"We, as in *us*." Haley pointed at them in a circle. "Plus the guys. And we're going out as in to some grownup bars." Haley wasn't letting their scarce enthusiasm damper hers. "We're finally all twenty-one. You know what that means."

Madison scoffed. "I'd rather not be the fifth wheel. Thanks, but no thanks."

"Madison!" Haley turned to face her. "You wouldn't be the fifth wheel. A lot of guys from the team are coming. The season is over, and they can finally enjoy their Saturdays like normal people. You could meet someone."

"Yeah, sure," Madison said. "Because that always happens to me."

Madison's neck and cheeks heated; she'd hidden the real reason for not wanting to go behind sarcasm. So far, Alice reflected, her friend had never seen Haley and Scott together. Madison had probably gone out of her way to make sure that didn't happen.

As for Peter and Alice, this was the first weekend after the season's end—excluding spring break—that they could go out together. Even with Haley dating Scott for three months, there hadn't been any previous group dates. A beer with Peter and a random guy or guys on the team on weekdays at the most. But the basketball season *was* over, and change was in the air…

"Is Jack included in the group?" Alice asked, to draw attention away from sulking Madison.

"I'm not sure, but most of the team is going," Haley replied.

"David, too?" Alice asked.

Haley shrugged. "Probably."

Madison threw her a mean stare. "It must be nice having two guys fighting over you."

Haley frowned. "As it happens, it's pretty horrible. What's up with you? Did you eat lemons for breakfast?"

Madison caught herself and blushed a deeper shade of red. "I'm sorry, Haley, it's not you." It was clear to Alice how Madison was trying her best not to be jealous or bitter, but sometimes her repressed feelings got the best of her. "I just got a low grade and can't wrap my head around why."

Haley rolled her eyes. "What did you get, a B+?"

"A-, actually. But I really can't understand why the minus."

Haley turned to Alice. "Are you going to smack her, or should I?"

"Hey," Madison protested. "I'm right here. I can hear you."

Haley blew out air. "So, tonight. Are we on?"

"Sure," Alice said.

"I guess," Madison agreed.

"Great!" Haley clapped her hands twice. "I'll call Scott and organize everything."

While Haley was busy on the phone with her boyfriend, Alice whispered, "Are you okay? You don't have to come if you don't want to."

Madison's lips parted in a sad smile. "I have to face them sooner or later. I won't be able to avoid them forever."

"Okay," Alice continued in hushed tones. "But if it gets too much, let me know. Promise?"

Madison nodded.

***

The downtown bar Haley had chosen was already half full when the three of them strolled inside. It was fancy in an urban way: brick walls with wide, metal-framed windows and high ceilings. Tall, circular tables surrounded a dais in the center of the room.

None of the guys had arrived yet, so the girls got started on cocktails. With her birthday in mid-December, Haley still wasn't over the thrill of legally ordering a drink in a public space. She immediately offered to go order for everyone. They happily let her.

"How are you holding up?" Alice asked Madison.

She grimaced. "You don't have to check on me every five seconds. I can handle myself."

From the way Madison kept gnawing her bottom lip, eyes glued to the entrance door, Alice doubted her friend was going to handle anything well. But she didn't press her further. Haley came back with their drinks and started babbling about something. Alice didn't listen. She was too distracted worrying about Madison.

Haley snapped her fingers in both their faces. "Hey, I'm talking. What's up with you two?"

"Nothing," Alice and Madison said in unison.

After being caught, they both made an effort to act normal and give Haley their undivided attention. At least, until Madison went suddenly pale. Her gaze fixed over Alice's shoulder with that deer-in-headlights expression. Alice turned toward the front of the pub where the heads of several tall guys bobbed above the crowd, heading toward them. Her eyes trained on Jack first, then Peter, Scott, and the many other familiar faces with them. It looked like Haley had been right; most of the team was here. At least everyone old enough for public drinking.

Peter greeted her with a kiss, and Scott did the same with Haley. Madison stared, petrified.

"Hi, babe," Haley said to Scott. "Remember Alice?"

Scott looked at her and said, "Hi."

"And this is Madison," Haley continued. "My other roommate."

A flicker of recognition creased Scott's forehead. "Hi." He smiled as if he'd placed where he'd seen her. "You're in my poetry class."

"Yeah." To her credit, Madison managed to function as a normal human being, smiling only a little awkwardly. "Madison, nice to meet you."

"Scott."

They shook hands, and when Scott turned to kiss Haley again, Madison downed her entire drink. Alice was about to say something when she became distracted by Jack appearing with a flock of girls in tow. They looked like freshmen at best, but they couldn't be. In a bar, it always was twenty-one-and-above only. Fake IDs, perhaps? Jack was shamelessly flirting with three of them at the same time, and he was clearly well on his way to charming the pants off the entire group.

Alice sighed and then followed Madison's lead, downing her drink in one sorry gulp.

Twenty-nine
Madison

"Oh, look," Madison muttered into her glass, talking to herself. "Haley is going home with Scott. *Super fun!*" She stared at the half-consumed drink in her hand, waiting for a reply, and decided it was better to finish her cocktail rather than trying to talk with it. Madison tilted her head backward and chugged. What in the hell had made her agree to come out with *them* tonight?

Two hours into the evening and Madison was ready to call it quits. She'd masochistically stalked Haley and Scott most of the night and had had enough. If Haley—who had insisted so much on this "night out drinking," only to sip a single cocktail and ignore her friends to be with her boyfriend—was going home, so could Madison. She had drunk enough to be tipsy, and the constant thumping in her temples promised a mean hangover the next day.

Madison was about to follow the happy couple out when another member of the team leaned his elbows on the table next to her now-empty glass. "They make my stomach turn, too," he said.

Madison detached her gaze from Scott and Haley to stare up at the newcomer. To call him "hot" would have been an understatement. "And you are?" she asked.

"David. Pleased to meet you." He smiled a confident, lopsided grin that screamed *danger*.

Madison's lips parted in a surprised O. "You're the infamous brother." It figured that Scott's brother would be even better looking and into Haley just as much as his younger sibling.

"I hope you didn't believe everything you heard about me."

"Why?" Madison cocked her head to the side. "I've only heard good things. Are they not true?"

Whoops, she was flirting. *So?* David looked just as pissed off at the leaving duo as she was; so what if they mourned together?

Trouble shared is a trouble halved.

David jerked his chin toward her empty glass. "Want another one of those?"

"Sure, why not?"

Or possibly double-trouble.

"You go to Harvard too?" David asked, once he was back with their drinks.

"Yep," Madison said between sips. "What's your concentration?"

"Statistics. Yours?"

"Ew. No offense, but I can't stand numbers."

David smiled genially. "None taken."

"I'm studying English Literature and Poetry."

David raised his eyebrows. "I hope you're not as much of a tormented soul as my little brother."

Madison blushed at the mention of Scott. "I hope 'tormented' isn't the first word that comes to mind when one looks at me."

"Definitely not." Davis brushed his right thumb across her cheek. "'Beautiful' would be more appropriate."

The rosy tint on her cheeks grew a deeper red. "Want to dance?" Madison asked, for lack of other responses.

David pinned her with his blue gaze. “I’d love to.”

“Great!”

Madison gulped down the remains of her drink and grabbed David’s hand to lead him to the dais in the center of the room. It was already crowded with throngs of partygoers having a good time. She made to turn to face David, but he spun her round and wrapped his arms around her from behind. As they started swaying in time to the music, David’s chin brushed the top her head. He was so tall. Having him so close, Madison moved rigidly as a stick at first. Until David lowered his head and whispered, “Relax,” close enough to her ear to send shivers down her spine.

Maybe it was the one-too-many drinks, or the hot guy standing behind her, or the one that had gone home with her best friend. Madison didn’t care; she let her inhibitions melt away. She was happy to just dance to the fast rhythm of the music, pressing herself against the solid wall of David’s chest. She lost count of how many songs played before the dancing changed to full-scale making out. David was a great kisser.

Her phone started vibrating in her small leather clutch. Madison ignored it, too engrossed in the kiss to stop. But when it kept on vibrating, she pulled back with an embarrassed, “Sorry” to check out who it was.

She had two missed calls and a text from Alice asking where she was and saying she was heading home.

“It’s Alice,” Madison said. “She’s going home. You want to go, too?”

David smiled. “I’m having fun right here.”

"Yeah, me too. Do you mind waiting here while I go say bye?"

"Not at all." David grabbed her by the waist and pulled her close to kiss her lightly on the lips. "Don't make me wait too long."

Madison blushed. "I won't." She took two steps backward, never breaking eye contact, and turned to push her way through the crowd to go tell Alice she was staying.

Thirty
Haley

Haley left Scott's apartment early the next morning. She had a ton of homework to do before Monday and an entire program to code that she'd left to the last minute. Scott walked her halfway to a Starbucks, where they had breakfast together, and then kissed her goodbye. Haley sleepwalked the rest of the way home; the coffee had not been strong enough to wake her up properly. Mercifully, it took her only five minutes to get to her building and take the elevator up to her floor.

Pushing open the door to her apartment, Haley was startled to find a tall, dark-haired, bare-backed guy in her kitchen. Haley couldn't see his bottom half from behind the bar, but she hoped at least that part was covered up. The mysterious dude was standing in front of their opened fridge, acting as if he owned the place. The mere stance of his shoulders exuded arrogance. He took his time to examine the contents of the fridge and settled on Haley's 2% milk. With the milk carton in his hands, the dude grabbed a glass out of the cabinet above the sink and poured himself a drink.

The theft of her milk shook Haley out of her shock. She kicked the entrance door shut with force, to make sure it made enough noise to startle the thief. *It did.* As the door slammed shut, the dude's shoulders jerked. But the milk thief didn't turn around. He finished drinking his milk, taking his time, and then placed the used glass in the sink without washing it.

Haley's nostrils flared. "That's my milk you're drinking," she accused.

Slowly, deliberately he turned around, and Haley found herself staring into a pair of piercing blue eyes. *David.*

"Morning, Sunshine," he purred. His lips parted in a lopsided grin. "I apologize for abusing your hospitality." He made a mock bow. "I'll buy you a new carton."

Haley narrowed her eyes to slits. "What are you doing in my house?" she hissed.

"I'm a guest."

"I never invited you here."

"*You* are not the only person living here."

His eyes never left hers, causing a soft blush to creep up her cheeks.

"What do you mean?" she asked, even if a sneaking suspicion was already making her heart beat faster.

"Your roommate is a lovely girl," David said. He walked out from behind the bar.

Please let him not be naked, please let him not be naked, Haley chanted in her head.

He rounded the corner, revealing that he was wearing the same pants he'd had on last night. Haley was both relieved and somehow disappointed at his being half-dressed. Before she could stop herself, her eyes traveled down his chest and over his sculpted stomach, coming to rest just above the open button of his pants.

"See something you like?" he asked, cocking one eyebrow.

"*No.*"

David closed the distance between them until he was so near Haley could feel the heat coming from his body. "I'll see you later, then." He gave her that mocking grin again. "Or not."

Haley poked him just below the collarbone, pressing hard on his chest. "Hurt her and—"

"What?" he challenged, inching even closer, his face a breath away from hers. "What are you going to do, Princess?"

Haley held his gaze. "You don't want to find out," she hissed.

David stepped backward. "Relax," he said. "Contrary to popular belief, I can be a gentleman when the need calls for it." Without waiting for a reply, David walked into Madison's room and closed the door behind him.

Haley was left standing alone in the hall, her face so hot she was sure she must've had steam coming out her ears. She glared at Madison's door, then stormed inside her own room.

Throwing her coat on the bed, she searched her bedroom for something that would help distract her. Haley sat at her desk, stabbed the "on" button of her laptop, and opened a blank C++ page. Programming always calmed her, but today it was life or death. It'd keep her from bursting into Madison's room to drag the bastard out by his hair.

With one hand clenched on the mouse and the other drumming on the wooden desk, Haley tried to focus on the program. The blinking cursor teased her, waiting to be moved, making her brain feel as empty as the blank page. David's smug smirk kept appearing in her mind's eye, erasing everything else. She couldn't remember the simplest input command. When squealing giggles echoed in the adjoining room, Haley's concentration failed, and her mood blackened even more. This David situation was not working for her; she had to do something to stop him.

***

Haley remained in her room until she was sure that both David and Madison had left the apartment. Not that it did her any good. She hadn't accomplished anything the entire morning and was still fuming from her short encounter with David. When it seemed safe to come out, Haley tiptoed into the living room, still wary of her own house. Alice was sitting at the dining table doing homework.

Haley strolled toward her. "We need to talk."

"Hey." Alice lifted her head from her chemistry book. "I didn't know you were home."

Haley sat in the chair opposite to her. "Did you know who else was here?"

"Yeah."

From her tone, Alice didn't seem too happy either.

"How did it happen?" Haley asked.

Alice dropped her pen and closed her book, resting her elbows on it. "After you left with Scott, I went home with Peter. Madison told me she was having fun, and that she was staying. I didn't know that it was David providing the entertainment and charming his way to her bedroom."

"What do you think about it?" Haley asked.

Alice leaned back in her chair, crossing her arms. "What do *you* think? You seem to have a definite opinion on the subject."

Haley lowered her gaze and bit her bottom lip. She was ashamed of her train of thought.

"Come on," Alice encouraged. "Spit it out."

Haley scrunched her face. "Promise you won't judge me?"

"Why would I?"

"What I am about to say is horrible, and you might think I'm a presumptuous bitch."

Alice smiled reassuringly. "I'm sure I won't."

"Okay." Haley inhaled, and prepared to say the unsayable all in one breath without pausing. "I think David is sleeping with Madison only because he wants to mess with me to make me jealous. I'm not saying Madison is not likable or anything; she's absolutely likable. I just don't think *he* likes her. Am I the most arrogant person in the world and the worst friend ever for thinking that?"

Alice shook her head. "No. Unfortunately, I agree with you. I don't like David. Something about him is off, and he's taking advantage of Madison. But I'm not sure why."

"Do we tell her?"

"NO!" Alice shouted. "Never. You can never say anything about it to Madison."

Haley had not expected a reaction so strong. "Whoa, relax. Why can't we talk to her?"

"I'm sorry for yelling at you," Alice apologized. "It's just that Madison is already so insecure around guys. We can't put more doubts in her head. She looked so happy this morning."

Haley felt like gagging. "I'm glad I didn't see that." David's behavior was literally making her stomach ache.

"So what do we do? We tell the guys to do an intervention on his side?"

"Why?" Alice asked skeptically. "You think he would listen?"

"No, probably not."

"And I wouldn't put it past him to tell Madison."

"You're right..." Haley suppressed a frustrated scream. "We can't sit here and watch him play with Madison's heart. So?"

"I'm sorry, but that's exactly what we do: *nothing*."

"Nothing? How can—"

"Haley," Alice interrupted. "I know you're worried. I am, too. But if we try to do something, anything at all, we'd be playing his game. He'd use it to hurt Madison or you, try to get between you two. Ignore David long enough and you'll be calling his bluff."

"I hate sitting here doing nothing!"

"I know." Alice reached across the table to grab her hand. "But it's the right thing to do."

"I hate him." Haley squeezed her friend's hand. "I was giving him the benefit of the doubt, but now..." She shook her head. "I hate him."

"It's hard to think he's Scott's brother."

"Yeah, right? Now Hawaii makes a lot more sense. Imagine having to put up with him your entire life."

"Poor Scott," Alice agreed.

"Let's talk about something else." Haley let go of Alice's hand to pull one foot up on the chair and hug a knee to her chest. "Is everything all right with you and Peter? You've seemed off lately."

A dark shadow crossed Alice's face. "Wrong topic."

"Okay. So what was up with Jack last night? He was flirting with all breathing things."

Alice's cheeks heated up. "Even more wrong topic."

"Why? You're not still into him, are you?"

Alice stared her down. "Haley, I love you, but this is your third strike."

"But you've been with Peter for how many months now—?"

"I'm not talking about it, so drop it," Alice hissed. Then, regaining her cool, she added, "Can we talk about something not boy-related?"

The two of them stared at each other blankly.

Alice cracked first, bursting out laughing. "Look at us," she chuckled. "We're two promising, bright Harvard students and all we can talk about is guys."

"If you want, we can discuss the latest Kardashian drama," Haley said genially.

Alice scowled at her, still smirking. "I'd rather not. How about we just do our homework?"

"Fine!"

Haley pushed her chair back and went to retrieve her laptop, ready to spend the rest of the day brooding.

Thirty-one

Alice

Haley's mood did not improve over the next few weeks. Alice kept catching her walk around the house with pursed lips and a morose frown. Madison was at the opposite end of the emotional spectrum. She waltzed through the apartment with a happy, distracted air.

Alice was torn. She was happy Madison was taking a break from her heartache over Scott and Haley. But her dating David was an awful idea. To discuss the issue with Haley was out of the question. Her other roommate wasn't aware of the full extent of the problem. Haley kept insisting on an intervention whenever the subject came up, which was a no-no. Only two other people knew everyone involved: Peter and Jack. Alice had to open up with one of them or she would go mad. But which one?

Alice stared at the ceiling of her room, trying to ignore her inner voice which screamed for her to confide in Jack. It was getting harder every day. Her relationship with Peter had been deteriorating ever since spring break. On the outside, everything seemed fine. Deep down, the excitement had worn off and their differences were becoming too evident to be set aside much longer.

A sudden bang made Alice jolt in her bed, and Blue went running under the bed, squealing in terror. Alice hopped off and tiptoed to her door to check out what was going on outside. Madison and David were standing in the entrance hall kissing.

Alice cleared her throat. "What's going on?"

Madison broke the kiss and David answered, "Darling Haley seems to be in a mood." He looked smug and self-satisfied.

Alice narrowed her eyes at him. "I wonder why."

David shrugged innocently.

Madison threw her a questioning look. "Is something wrong with Haley?"

"No," Alice lied. "Have fun, guys. I'll see you later." She disappeared back into her room before Madison could ask more questions.

***

"Can we go somewhere private to talk?" Alice asked Jack as they exited their last lecture the next day.

His mouth gaped open before he asked, "Am I in trouble?"

"No." Alice smiled. "Not you."

"Where do you want to go?"

"Somewhere no one can overhear us."

"Secret stuff, huh?" Jack grinned. "How about the Chem Lab?"

"We're not allowed in there."

"Neither is anyone else; it's the perfect place for secret meetings."

"All right, but if we get caught and kicked out of school, you get to explain it to my dad. Deal?"

"Deal."

They walked down the hall furtively and waited for the hall to be empty before sneaking inside the lab. Alice sat on the teacher's desk and Jack stood before her with an expectant frown. Glass beakers, vials, and jars of powdered ingredients surrounded them.

"It's Madison," Alice said, and for just a second, she could've sworn Jack paled. "She's sleeping with David."

Jack raked his hand through his hair. *Was that relief on his face?*

"I assume that's bad news?" he asked.

Alice drummed her heels on the desk's wooden panel. "What do you think?"

"David's on the team, but we don't hang much. He's a loner."

"Exactly my point."

"Yeah, but you haven't dragged me to a secret meeting just to tell me this, right?"

"No, there's more," Alice admitted. "But you have to promise you won't tell anyone. Deal?"

Jack made the Boy Scout salute. "Deal."

"Madison is secretly in love with Scott."

"David's brother?"

"Yeah, Haley's boyfriend, too," Alice clarified. "Haley doesn't know, and she can't find out."

"Okay."

"But we think—Haley and I, that is—that David is only using Madison to screw with Scott and Haley."

Jack scratched his head. "And you concluded this how?"

"David tried to make a pass at Haley several times; it seems too much of a coincidence for him to date our roommate next."

Jack was not convinced. "Why would he do it?"

"To make Haley jealous."

"That would work only if Haley... I mean, is she?

Jealous?"

"She won't admit it, but I think she is a little." Alice nodded. "David has a unique way of getting under Haley's skin."

"So his diabolical plan is working." Jack let out a mocking evil laugh.

Despite the seriousness of the discussion, Alice chuckled. "Yeah, Haley is brooding half the time. But it's Madison that's the real problem." Alice's cheeks heated with worry. "She's so insecure around guys, and she's only ever dated d-bags. You know, the type who only use her for cheap one-night stands. Madison can't know David is using her, too. And if he breaks her heart…"

Jack looked away as if he was embarrassed. Was he self-conscious about treating women poorly? *He should be.*

"Is this too much girl talk for you?" Alice asked.

"No." He met her eyes again, still wary. "But I don't see what your point is."

"I need advice." Alice groaned. "What would you do in my place? If Haley and Madison were your friends."

Jack thought a while. "Honestly? Nothing," he said.

Alice breathed in relief at Jack coming to the same conclusion she had.

"If David only wants to make Haley jealous," Jack continued, "and she does nothing, this little act will become boring for him in no time. The best advice I can give you is to tell Haley to act as happy as she can around David, instead of letting him know she's pissed off."

"Yeah, you're right. I'll do exactly that." Alice hopped off the desk. "Thanks for listening."

Jack pulled her into a hug. She wished she never had to let him go.

***

Back home, Alice tapped on Haley's door and slipped inside without waiting for permission.

"Can I talk to you?" she whispered.

"Why are we whispering?" Haley used the same hushed tones.

"Because I don't want Madison to overhear us."

Haley beckoned her to the bed where she was already under the covers with her laptop on her knees. "What's up?" she asked.

"David."

"What did he do?" Haley hissed, making room for Alice on the bed.

"Nothing." Alice paused. "Nothing new, I mean."

"So?"

"It's you."

Haley mouthed, "Me?"

"Yeah, you," Alice confirmed. "You can't glower at him every time you see him around the house."

"But—"

"And you can't disappear into your room and slam the door when you catch them kissing, either."

Haley pouted.

"I know you're mad." Alice squeezed her friend's knee. "But right now you're right where he wants you, and David knows it."

Haley chewed her lower lip. "So what do I do?"

"When you see them, smile, be pleasant… act as if you don't care…"

"But I do care."

"Which is why you have to do this."

"You're right. I've been an ass." Haley pursed her lips in a determined expression. "I'll fake-please the shit out of him."

"That's my girl talking." Alice stared at her watch. "Gosh, it's late." She yawned. "I said my piece, I'll go."

Haley pulled her into a hug. "Thank you for the tough love."

"You're welcome." Alice got up. "Night."

"Night."

Alice sneaked out of Haley's room as silently as she had walked in and tiptoed across the hall. She headed to her room, but changed her mind mid-course and paused in front of Madison's door. *Hell, in for a penny, in for a pound.* It was time for a second pep talk.

Again, Alice gave a soft knock and slunk in, uninvited.

"Hey, do you have a minute?" she whispered.

Madison closed a book and looked up at her. "Why are you whispering?"

Alice made her way to the bed. "I don't want Haley to overhear us."

Deja vù, anyone?

Madison frowned. "I have a feeling I won't like the next thing that's going to come out of your mouth. What is it?"

Alice decided to cut straight to the chase. "Scott. Why are you dating his brother?"

"Why not?"

"Isn't it weird that one minute you like Scott, and the next you're dating within the same gene pool?"

"Scott is with Haley," Madison replied, annoyed.

"Yeah, for now."

"Are you suggesting I should save myself for Scott in case one day they break up?" Madison sounded bitter.

"That's not what I meant."

"What, then?"

"I'm just saying that, considering your feelings for Scott, it could be a bad idea to date his brother." *His bastard of a brother, more accurately.*

"I don't have feelings for Scott."

Okay, Madison was in full-blown denial.

Alice crossed her arms and arched an eyebrow at her friend.

Madison dropped the book she'd been reading on the nightstand and leaned forward on the bed, reaching for Alice's hands. "Listen, I had a silly crush on Scott, but that's over." Alice wasn't convinced but let Madison finish, anyway. "Before Haley introduced us, we hadn't spoken once. He was the cute guy in my class I liked to look at and fantasize about."

"So it was never something serious?" Alice asked, still skeptical.

"Just a fantasy."

"And David? Are you guys serious?"

"It's early days." Madison smiled, and Alice had to master all her self-control not to flinch. "I don't know what's going to happen."

"Please be careful, okay?"

"Why?"

Alice shrugged. "Scott seems like a good guy, and he hates his brother."

"Does that make David a villain?"

"No, it just puts him on my watch-list."

"You're so scary," Madison joked.

Alice lifted her hands, scrunched her face, and let out a terrifying zombie growl.

Madison chuckled.

Alice patted the bed. "I'll let you get back to your book." She made to get up, but Madison pulled her back onto the bed.

"Wait a second," Madison said. "Now it's time for pep talk number two."

Three, actually. Alice was surprised, so she asked, "What did I do?"

"What's going on with you and Peter?"

Alice groaned. "It's too late to have this conversation."

It was Madison's turn to arch an eyebrow.

"Okay," Alice said. "What do you want to know?"

"Are you in love with your boyfriend?"

Alice didn't have to think for a second. "No."

"Then what are you doing with him?"

"It helps with other things…"

Madison did not relent. "Like pretending you have no feelings for Jack?"

Alice ignored the question. "I should've never come into your room."

"Too late for that."

"What do you want me to say?"

Madison leaned back against the headboard. "I don't want you to say anything. Just listen for once."

"Go ahead." Alice rolled her eyes. "Say your piece."

"I'm not touching the Jack topic for now," Madison started.

"Thank you for your clemency," Alice said in a worshipping voice. "Oh, sage roommate."

Madison ignored the jibe. "So, Peter. When you started going out with him, he made you happy. Everyone could tell. But lately…"

"Is it so obvious?"

"For people that know you? Yes." Madison confirmed the fears that had been gnawing at Alice's side since spring break. "What happened?"

"In the beginning, it was new and exciting." Alice stared blankly into the past before concentrating on Madison's worried eyes. "Lately, I'm realizing how different we are. I mean, spring break was a nightmare. We're so different. We only work..." Alice blushed. "Physically. Everything else feels off."

"Why are you still with him, then?" Madison pinned her with a stare. "Were you hoping the school year would end and you wouldn't have to break up with Peter because he would just move away?"

Nailed it. "Is that bad?"

"Duh!" Madison made a silly face. "It's always better to have a clean cut."

Alice shook her head. "I came here to dispense my wisdom, and you kicked me in the butt instead." She pouted. "Now I'm going to go mope alone in my room." Alice stood up and Madison didn't stop her this time.

She laughed. "You do that."

Alice waved goodbye. "Night."

"Night."

Alice returned to her room and collapsed on her bed with a heavy sigh. Talk about food for thought—between her roommates' love lives and her own, she had enough thinking material for ages.

Thirty-two
Alice

Alice stared in the mirror. A plain white t-shirt, a pair of light-wash jeans, and white sneakers seemed like an appropriate breakup outfit. Lectures were over and, with Peter's graduation looming over them, Alice wanted to end their story before finals week. Peter had been a whirlwind of excitement in her life, but their relationship wasn't forever and ever. It had never been.

In the past month and a half, Alice had kept appearances up. It had been easier to pretend everything was fine than to face up to her real feelings. Now it was time to grab the Chicago Bull by the horns. It was only a matter of time before he moved to Illinois, anyway; his agent had been super positive about the Bulls making an offer. There was no point in staying together. It was only a matter of who said it first.

Now that she thought about it, this would be the first time Alice was doing the dumping. In all her previous relationships, even when she'd known things weren't going well, she'd always allowed the other person to call the shots. Not this time. Strangely, the prospect of being single didn't make her feel insecure. Alice wasn't scared of being alone anymore. Was this what growing up meant?

She knew calling it off with Peter was the right thing to do. That fact didn't help her lack of experience in breaking the news, however. She'd done an extensive Google search on the dos and don'ts of the process. After being on the receiving end so many times, Alice should've been much more of an expert, but right now her mind felt blank. Honestly, there had never been a breakup modus operandi that had made her feel better about what was happening. She did a mental recap of the Internet's advice all the same. The main dos were to tell him before anyone else (Madison didn't count), to be one-hundred percent sure and honest—but not brutal—and to do it in person. She had that covered. The don'ts included not using empty clichés, not asking for a "break," and, apparently, public spaces were a huge no-no. That's why Alice had asked Peter if she could drop by his house later, *yes,* and if his roommate was going to be there, *no.*

Peter opened the door to his house with a smile so dashing, a little something fluttered in Alice's belly. A million doubts immediately attacked her brain, and she tried to chase them away. A strong physical attraction wasn't enough to stay with a guy.

"Hey." He pulled her into a crushing hug.

"Hey, yourself."

Peter let her inside the house, whistling a happy tune.

"You're in a good mood?" Alice asked guiltily; she was about to ruin that for him.

"Oh, baby, you've no idea. I just got *the* call." He stared at the ceiling. "I'm in."

Alice could tell his mind was a million miles away.

"In…?"

"The NBA." He cupped her face and stamped a kiss on her lips. "A two-year contract."

"That's great." *And also the perfect excuse.* "Where, Chicago?"

Peter did a stupid, hip-hop victory dance. "Yep."

"Amazing." Alice's smile tensed. This was the perfect moment to tell him.

"What's up, baby? You look so serious."

Alice sat on the couch. "Can we talk for a minute?"

Peter looked at her warily. "All right." He sat next to her.

"This year with you has been… the most exciting of my life, and I'm glad I've gotten to know you…"

Peter's face darkened. "But?"

"But you're moving to Chicago. You'll have this electrifying new life and I'm super happy for you, I am, but I'm staying here. You'll be traveling a lot, meeting so many people. I'm not going to fit in that life, and I guess we've always known this—us—wasn't forever."

Peter remained silent for a second, then said, "Be honest, Alice. We'd be having this conversation even if Chicago wasn't in the picture, right?"

"True," Alice admitted. Peter was so sharp sometimes. "Listen." The next part was the hard one. "I love spending time with you, and we have a great chemistry, but…" She paused. "I'm not in love with you. And you aren't with me, either, are you?"

The L-word had not made an appearance in the six months they'd dated.

"I'm not sure." Peter looked crestfallen. "You're the first girl I really liked."

"That's because I'm super awesome," Alice tried to joke, but she felt choked. Saying goodbye wasn't easy, no matter how sure she was. "If you were in love with me, you'd be sure. It isn't something you can half-feel."

"I've never been in love, so I wouldn't know. Have you?"

Yes, with Jack. I still am. Alice blushed. "Only once, and it sucked." *It still sucks.*

"*This* sucks," Peter complained. "I didn't think we would say goodbye today."

"But you knew we would, eventually?"

"Yes, I guess I did." Peter opened his arms. "Come here." He pulled her onto his lap, and she nestled her chin on his shoulder. "I know you're right, baby," he said, stroking her hair. "It's just that I'll miss you."

"Me too." Alice sniffed. "But it's not like we're breaking up because we hate each other. We can always keep in touch." She pulled back to look at him.

He seemed to consider but shook his head. "Nah, we both know it wouldn't work."

"No, probably not. I have no past experiences to relate to. You're the first ex I'd like to keep in touch with." Alice fought back tears. "But you'll be too busy fending off cheerleaders and fans, anyway."

Peter's eyes were so blue, and his face so gorgeous. He wasn't making this easy on her.

"Can't we keep seeing each other until we're both in Boston?" he asked.

For a moment, Alice was tempted to say yes. What difference would a month make? But it'd only be a slower death—what was the point?

"I couldn't stand it." She shook her head. "It'd be like going around with a stick of dynamite and a ticking clock attached to our backs. It'd be horrible."

"You're right. A clean cut is best." Peter stood up, scooping her into his arms and carrying her with him. "But don't think for a minute I won't see to you one last time."

Alice giggled and let him take her to his room. Ah well, give it to Peter to know how to say goodbye in style. *Best. Breakup. Ever.*

Thirty-three

Alice

The school year was over. Finals were over. After exiting their last exam, Alice and Jack strolled around campus enjoying the warm mid-May sun on their faces. As they headed across Cambridge Common Park, Alice recognized Rose and Tyler talking on a bench nearby. They were immersed in conversation, both their faces dead serious. Should she text Georgiana?

Alice decided to mind her own business. She grabbed Jack's arm to pull him back. "Do you mind if we go the other way?"

Jack cut her a surprised look. "No, why?"

"No reason."

Jack looked unconvinced but didn't press her, so they headed in the opposite direction toward Harvard Yard. They wandered around aimlessly for a while, mostly in silence, until they stopped for a Frappuccino. Jack walked in to get their drinks and Alice waited at a table outside. It took him only five minutes to order and join her.

Alice studied him. He'd been fidgeting in a nervous way all day, and it wasn't like him to stare into space as he was doing now. Maybe before an exam, when he was mentally studying, but definitely not after. He was acting as if he was rehearsing a speech in his head.

"Something on your mind?" Alice asked.

Jack's eyes flickered to her face, troubled, before he looked ahead and spoke, "Ice, I know you're with Peter and

I shouldn't say anything—"

"We broke up."

His face whipped toward hers so fast she was afraid his neck would snap. "Really? When?"

"Two weeks ago."

"That long." Jack seemed hurt she hadn't told him.

"He didn't tell you?"

"With the season over we don't hang out that much." Jack shrugged. "How did it…? I thought you…"

"Loved him?" Alice finished the phrase for him. "No. Peter is fun, but I don't love him. There's only so far you can go in a relationship if you don't love someone. We lacked the spark."

"So it wasn't because of the NBA? Matt told me about the Bulls."

Alice smiled mischievously. "Actually, that gave me the perfect excuse to break up. The long distance scenario, and how it would've never worked."

Jack blinked. "You mean *you* broke up with him?"

"Yeah. Don't look that surprised. And don't worry, he wasn't too heartbroken or anything." Alice paused, gathering the courage to ask, "What about you? Any new girl on the horizon?"

"No, no one. I haven't found my spark either."

Jack looked at Alice as if there was more he wanted to say.

"Well, it must be hard." She chuckled awkwardly. "My roommates and I are probably the only three girls on campus you haven't slept with."

Why did she always have to blab stupid things when she was nervous?

Jack's neck flushed scarlet and his jaw tensed. "Right."

Alice frowned. "Why did you blush just now?"

"I didn't." He flashed her a dismissive grimace.

"Yes, you did. I told you my roommates and I are the only three people on campus you haven't had sex with, and your neck turned fifty shades of red."

Jack lowered his gaze to the floor. He looked guilty, like someone who'd been caught. But caught at what?

"Oh gosh," Alice gasped, bringing a hand to her mouth, realization washing over her. No, it couldn't be true! She felt tears welling in her eyes and she, too, stared at the floor. "Haley or Madison?" she whispered.

"It was nothing."

"Haley. Or. Madison?" Alice repeated through gritted teeth, keeping her gaze trained on her sneakers.

"Madison."

A blade cut through Alice's heart. "When?"

"It was a one night stand at the beginning of freshman year; she wasn't your roommate then, and I didn't know you knew each other."

Alice did a mental timeline of her friendship with Madison. They'd met as pledges at Kappa Kappa Gamma. But they hadn't become close friends until toward the end of freshman year when they'd moved in together. Alice hadn't told Madison about her crush on Jack until several months later. *Still.* At one point Madison must have realized.

Fighting back the tears, Alice said, "And the two of you just happened to both forget to tell me you'd slept together?" Alice waited for a sob to die in her throat before she continued. "What did you have, a secret meeting agreeing not to say anything?"

"No, you know I would never—"

Alice glared at him, not caring that her eyes were probably bloodshot by now. "No, Jack, at this point I don't know."

He paled and whispered, "I think we both decided it wasn't worth discussing."

"Mmm, usually people keep secrets about things that matter." Anger was mounting inside Alice. "Not the other way around."

"Well, it didn't… matter. It wasn't that big of a deal."

"Sure. Nothing is ever a big deal with you."

"What's that supposed to mean?"

Jack's embarrassed face in the Chem Lab flashed before her eyes. "When we spoke in the Chem Lab, that's why you were so weird. I told you guys only ever used Madison for sex, and you were one of those guys." Alice wanted to gag. "And you said nothing!"

"What was I supposed to say? Yeah, I had sex with Madison once. So? Why are we arguing about Madison?" He slapped one hand on the table. "It was ages ago, and it meant nothing. Why are you so mad?"

"You still don't know, do you?" Alice turned her face away. "She's my best friend and you… you…"

"What?"

Alice couldn't keep her feelings bottled up inside any longer. She stared into his dark eyes and spilled it all out. "I'm in love with you, Jack. I have been since freshman year. I had to watch you go through girl after girl, and I hated every single one of them because I was jealous. I spent years hoping one day you'd notice me, or realize I wasn't just a good friend to talk to whenever you didn't have a date or someone to screw."

"Alice, I didn't know," Jack said pleadingly.

"Oh, I know *you* didn't know. But guess who did know?" People around them were staring, but Alice didn't care. "Try and guess one of the two people I confided in. Yeah, *Madison.* And all this time she never told me she had sex with you, and just by chance you never told me either." Alice stared at the sky, blinking. Gravity wasn't helping in keeping the tears in. Still looking up, she added, "I'm an idiot, but I'm not that stupid. I've probably been a running joke between the two of you this entire time."

Alice pushed her chair backward, making an angry scraping sound, and walked away as the first tears rolled down her cheeks.

Jack ran after her. "Alice." He grabbed her by the shoulders and forced her to turn. "I've been the idiot this entire time. You're the most wonderful person I know, and I should've realized a long time ago we weren't just friends." For an instant, the snake of Alice's hope lifted its head, ready to destroy all her rational thoughts as she waited for Jack to tell her that he felt the same, that he loved her. Instead, he added, "Madison was nothing."

Just like that, a mental image of her best friend naked in bed with Jack appeared before her eyes, and Alice couldn't take it. It made her so jealous her blood sizzled. Her stomach churned, and suddenly she was scared she might throw up.

"Nothing, huh?" she hissed, shoving Jack away.

He kept hold of her arm. "Ice, please."

"Let me go," Alice screamed, yanking her arm free. She turned on her heel and ran away, tears flying behind her in the wind and heavy sobs shaking her entire body.

Thirty-four
Madison

Madison was home alone. She was lounging on her twin bed reading a paper for class when a loud pounding on the apartment door startled her. The insistent sound of fists meeting with wood told her the noise wouldn't stop until whoever was out there was let in. And to have all that intensity, it had to be a male someone. She left her unfinished paper on the bed and went to open the door.

"Jack!" Madison was taken aback.

She barely had time to take in his crazed expression before Jack burst past her into the house, yelling, "Is she here?"

"Who? Alice?" Madison closed the door behind him. "I thought she was with you."

"She was."

Jack searched the apartment with his eyes as if he expected Alice to jump up from behind the couch and yell, "Surprise!"

Madison touched him gently on the back. "Jack, she isn't here."

Jack clenched his fists. "I need to find her!"

"What happened?"

Jack turned to face her. "She knows."

"Knows?" Madison frowned. "Knows what?"

"About us."

Madison suppressed a groan; she was scared and relieved all at once. The squashing weight of the secret was finally gone, but now the consequences of the truth were about to come back and bite her. Since the day Alice had pointed out her tall, brown-haired classmate as her crush, Madison had felt a gut-wrenching guilt. Every time Alice spoke about Jack, a stone settled in the pit of her stomach. Madison knew she should've told Alice she'd had sex with Jack the moment she'd recognized him, but she hadn't. She'd panicked instead. And after that first encounter, the more Madison kept quiet, the harder it became to talk. The fear of Alice shunning her, and of Haley choosing Alice over her, had been too much. For the first time in her life, Madison had met two girls she adored who wanted to be her friends. She didn't want Alice to hate her for something that had meant nothing, so she'd kept the secret. And so far, so had Jack.

Madison narrowed her eyes at him. "Why did you tell her?"

Jack raked a hand through his hair, his face tormented. "I didn't. It sort of… came out."

"How?" Madison hissed. *How could something this big "sort of" come out?*

Jack flinched. "She told me you three were the only girls on campus I hadn't slept with. When I didn't laugh along with her joke, she guessed the truth. It was one thing to not tell her, but when she asked me, I couldn't lie to her face."

"Oh." Madison covered her forehead with her hands. "Now she's going to hate me."

"Not as much as she hates me," Jack countered.

Madison didn't want to play the who-will-Alice-hate-more game. Jack had no idea why Alice was so upset. "You don't understand," Madison said.

"I do. She told me everything."

Madison doubted it. "Oh, really?"

"Yeah, really," Jack sneered. "She told me she's had feelings for me from the moment we met, and that she only ever told you and Haley. She said now it all felt like a bad joke. That we were having a laugh behind her back, or something."

It was worse than Madison thought. "Oh, no."

"I tried to tell her what happened with us meant nothing." Jack raised his hands defensively. "No offense."

Madison was well past the point of being stung by this comment. Their night together had meant nothing to her, either. Alice needed to understand that. As her mind raced to find ways to make Alice see the truth, Jack's last words penetrated her worried haze. Madison studied him. "Alice told you she was in love with you, and all you said was our night together was meaningless?"

"I didn't have time to tell her much else before she ran away. Any idea where she could be?"

"Maybe." Madison started pacing the room, thinking aloud. "There are a couple of places she could've gone to cool her head."

"Come on, give me directions so I can get going."

"No." Madison stepped back. "I need to explain everything to her first. Alice needs to be ready to listen to whatever you have to say."

"Madison." Jack's tone was low and his jaw tense. "I should speak to her first."

"Why? Because you did such a great job in the last conversation?"

"I don't need your permission," he snapped.

"No, but you need hers."

"Damn it!" Jack turned and punched the closest wall.

Madison jumped back, staring wide-eyed at the small dent Jack's fist had left in the drywall.

He wasn't moving now. He had his arms braced on the wall next to the dent, his shoulders heaving with forced breaths, and his head dropping low.

"Jack," Madison said. "Alice will need time before she's ready to talk to you."

He turned bloodshot eyes on her. "And what's different about you?"

"It's not the same."

"Why?"

"Because she isn't in love with me!"

Jack's jaw sagged. He closed and opened his mouth twice to retort, but nothing came out.

"You'd better go." Madison opened the apartment door and pushed a shocked-into-silence Jack out. "I'll ask Alice to call you, but you need to give her some space."

Jack didn't speak. With a dejected air, he turned on his heel and jogged down the hall. He would probably keep searching for Alice, but that wasn't Madison's concern right now. She shut the door and started pacing again. *What next?* She needed to find Alice and explain.

A minute later the door opened again and Haley shuffled into the house.

"Was that Jack I met in the hall?" Haley removed her jacket and hung it in the closet. "What was he doing here?"

Madison didn't answer. What would Haley think of her?

Haley gasped. "Is that a hole in my wall?"

A sob escaped Madison's lips.

"Mad, are you okay?" Haley dashed toward her. "Are you crying?"

Madison couldn't keep it together any longer; she hugged Haley and started crying. "It's bad, Haley, so bad," Madison wailed. "She will never forgive me."

"Who? Who has to forgive you, and why?" Haley pushed back to look at her. "Please sit down and tell me everything." Madison let Haley drag her to the couch. "What's going on?" Haley demanded.

Madison looked up at her friend and made her confession. "I slept with Jack."

"What?" Haley let go of her hands as if she was infected. "Now? *How could you?*"

"No, not now." Madison dropped her head into her hands. "Years ago, when we were freshmen. I didn't know you or Alice back then. I had no idea she liked him. But I never told her."

"Okay." Haley seemed to calm down. "Not as bad. So what was Jack doing here?"

"He told Alice." Madison straightened up and sobbed out the rest. "Apparently, Alice snapped and told him she was in love with him, that it was all a bad joke because I was one of the two people who knew and I never said anything."

"Mmm, I see why that could be a problem." Haley slumped back on the couch, pressing her palms to her eyes as if that could help her think.

The silence was unnerving. “Do you hate me?” Madison asked.

Haley lowered her hands and straightened up. “Of course not. You made a mistake is all.”

“Thank you.” Haley’s understanding meant the world. “What do I do now?”

“Find Alice and talk to her.” Haley made a huffing sound. “Where do we start?”

“I think she’s on the roof. She always goes there when she’s upset.”

“How do you know?”

“I just do.”

“See, you’re a much better friend than I am.”

“I’m sure Alice doesn’t feel that way right now.” Madison shook her head. “You want to come up with me?”

“Why?” Haley didn’t sound keen. “Isn’t it better if you talk alone?”

“I need you there to give an impartial, non-emotionally-involved perspective. And just in case she tries to throw me over the railing.”

Haley sighed and stood up. “Let’s go.”

Thirty-five
Alice

Alice leaned on the railing of her building's rooftop, staring at the Charles River and the Boston skyline in the distance. She wasn't really taking in the view; her mind was blank. All she could feel was the wind brushing against her face and pushing her tears backward. Mid-Spring and the late afternoon air was still cold in Cambridge.

Alice heard the rooftop's heavy metal door open and close. She didn't turn to look, but she was sure Madison had just walked outside. Her dear friend must have had another behind-her-back chat with Jack.

Still not turning, Alice said, "Go away. I don't want to see you."

"Alice, please, just hear me out," Madison pleaded.

Alice turned to face her ex-best friend and was surprised to find Haley standing beside Madison. She directed her fury at Haley first. "Did you know?"

Haley paled at the harshness of her tone. "No, I didn't. I swear."

Alice relaxed a little; at least she had *one* loyal friend who hadn't lied to her every day for the past two years. Haley approached her, and they hugged.

"I think you should hear Mad out," Haley whispered in her ear.

Alice pushed Haley back. "I don't care what she has to say."

"Alice, it meant nothing," Madison said.

"If I hear anybody else saying it meant nothing, I'm going to scream. People don't hide meaningless things; they hide the important stuff."

"But it wasn't important."

Alice narrowed her eyes. "So why keep it a secret?"

"I was scared you wouldn't want to be my friend any longer." Madison looked haggard: her face was red, blotchy, and covered in tears. The wind blowing against her made her appearance all the more tragic by giving her a halo of golden locks. But Alice wasn't about to be mollified by the act. "You'd just told me how deeply in love you were with Jack, and I didn't know what to do. I panicked. And after I didn't say anything that first time, it became harder and harder to tell you."

Excuses. These were all empty excuses. "Well, guess what? Now we're no longer friends. So there you go. Good job."

"Please don't say that." Madison sounded desperate.

"Alice," Haley said soothingly. "Maybe you should try to calm down."

"Why? She's a liar. She lied to you too, you know."

"To me?" Haley took a surprised step backward. "About what?"

"Alice, don't," Madison whimpered.

"She'll be after your boyfriend next." Alice knew she was being mean, but right now all she wanted was to hurt Madison as much as she'd hurt her.

"Scott?" Haley asked, moving her gaze back and forth from Alice to Madison. "What about Scott?"

"She likes him," Alice said.

Haley set her gaze on Madison. "Do you?"

"Yeah, I do. I did." Madison was becoming frantic. She was crying so hard she had trouble speaking. "But I would never try anything with your boyfriend, you have to know that. She's just being mean right now."

"How long have you liked him?" Haley asked. She didn't sound as mad as Alice had hoped.

"Forever," Madison confessed. "I told you he was in my English classes."

"So why didn't you say anything?"

"Because it doesn't matter!" Madison screamed. "It never matters. Scott doesn't want me. He never even noticed me before you started dating him. Guys never like me; they always like *you* or *you.*" Madison pointed at them each in turn. "Never me. So what was the point?"

"The point is being honest with your friends!" Alice yelled back.

Madison ignored Alice. "Haley, I never tried anything with Scott, and I never would. I'm with David."

Alice scoffed. "Yeah, about David—"

"Alice, shut up!" Haley froze her with a stare.

Alice's heart skipped a beat; she'd almost hurt Madison in such a way she'd never be able to take it back. But Madison wasn't stupid, and the withering look on Haley's face was too much of a giveaway.

"David what?" Madison asked.

Alice shrugged. "Nothing." She looked away, ashamed for what she'd almost said.

Haley kept silent.

"Who's keeping secrets now?" Madison asked.

No one replied.

"Fine!" Madison shouted. "You want to hate me for something that happened before I even knew you? Go ahead. Take the moral high ground because both of you are always so perfect. I'm out of here." Madison ran back to the door and disappeared down the stairs.

"That went well," Haley said, slapping her hands on the sides of her thighs. "Does she really like Scott? She told you?"

"She didn't have to, Haley." Alice rolled her eyes. "To anyone looking, it was pretty obvious from the first basketball game we watched."

Haley shook her head. "I never knew."

"I know. Subtle intuition isn't really your thing."

Alice walked back to the railing, and Haley followed her. "Is that a nice way to say I have my head stuck too high up my rear end?"

Alice chuckled coldly. "Let's say you're not the most observant person."

"Is that why she's sleeping with David?" Haley groaned. "That makes it even worse."

"I've no idea how her mind works. Believe me, I don't."

Haley kept quiet for a minute before saying, "Alice, what you were about to say—"

Alice didn't let her finish. "You don't have to tell me. Thank you for stopping me. I'm so mad, and I just wanted to hurt her…"

Haley sighed. "I get that she wasn't one-hundred percent honest, but—"

"It's Jack, Haley. Madison had sex with him." Alice kept imagining them together.

"Is the problem that she slept with him, or that she didn't tell you?"

"Both." Alice focused on the glistening water of the distant river, trying to let her eyes see only what was in front of her and not what her mind kept picturing. "I can't stand to look at her."

"Can you really blame her for not coming clean before?"

Alice turned to face Haley. "Why are you on her side?"

"I'm not," Haley hurried to say. "But can't you see she had a reason to be scared to tell you? Alice, your gut reaction is to hate her, and it would've been the same two years ago. Only now, you have a solid friendship that can take the hit. You didn't back then." Haley paused, most likely to give Alice time to process what she'd just said. "Can you honestly tell me it wouldn't have changed anything? She made a mistake because she was scared to lose you. Can't you forgive her?"

Alice shook her head. Madison was only half the coin of her emotional turmoil.

"What is it, Alice?" Haley insisted.

"I told him I loved him." Alice couldn't even say his name. "There's no taking it back this time."

"And how did he react? Did he say anything?"

"I can't remember." Alice wiped a tear from her cheek. "Something about Madison not being important. I'll have to change schools. I can't go here and see him every day for the next school year."

"That's a bit melodramatic." Haley waved a hand dismissively. "And finals are over, so you don't have to see

Jack for the entire summer if you don't want to. But you can't ignore Madison."

"Aren't you mad at her?" Alice asked.

"About Scott? Why would I be?"

"Why wouldn't you?" Alice insisted.

"Can't you see that not telling me she liked Scott was the most selfless thing to do?"

"How?"

"She could've called dibs on Scott," Haley explained. "But instead of having the 'I will have him or no one will' attitude, she let me date him. And I think she didn't want me to know about her feelings for him so that I wouldn't feel guilty about being with him."

"You make her sound like a saint," Alice said, resentful.

"What do you think was her motive? And why didn't *you* tell me?"

Alice had no other explanation for Haley's first question, so she ignored it and answered the second one. "It wasn't my secret to tell."

Haley crossed her arms and stared her down. "So there are secrets it's okay to keep, and others that are not?"

Alice hated when Haley was right. "I hate your cold logic."

"Do you hate Madison too?"

"No, not really," Alice admitted.

"Then you should let her off the hook." Haley walked away and beckoned Alice to follow. "Let's go downstairs so we can all talk without freezing our asses off."

***

When they entered Madison's room, it looked as if her wardrobe had vomited all her clothes on her bed. She had two suitcases open on the floor and she was scurrying between them and the bed, throwing in things at random.

Alice kept closer to the threshold, but Haley barged in, asking, "What are you doing?"

"I'm moving out," Madison said while she walked up and down, hauling clothes. "I'll stay at my parents' house, be out of your hair for good."

"Madison, stop!" Haley placed herself between the bed and the suitcases. "We don't want you to go."

Madison stopped and looked at Haley. "Aren't you mad at me?"

"No, of course not."

Madison popped her hip and propped a hand on her waist. "How come you don't care that I used to drool over your boyfriend?"

"For one," Haley said, "I know you never tried anything with him and never would. And I'm glad you allowed me to date him guilt-free."

Madison's lips parted in an astonished O-shape.

Alice followed the exchange, knowing it was her turn to absolve Madison next. As if on cue, Madison peeked at her over Haley's shoulder, her eyes still wide with fear.

"I don't want you to move out either," Alice said.

Madison went limp and collapsed to the floor. She landed in a sort of butterfly yoga pose and started ugly-crying again. "I'm sorry," she kept repeating between sobs. "I'm so sorry…"

She wasn't faking her pain. Something in Alice shifted; she sat on the floor next to her friend and hugged her. "I know," she said, stroking Madison's hair.

They did a Ping-Pong of respective apologies and half-choked sobs until Haley interrupted them. "Enough!" Haley was never one to dwell on sorrow. "This mess is not going to clean itself." She pointed at the cemetery of discarded clothes surrounding them. "Come on, you two." Haley offered them one hand each and pulled them up. "Madison, you take your things out of the suitcases. I'll put them back on hangers, and Alice, you hang them in the closet."

Alice found it helpful to concentrate on a practical task, and even if Madison still avoided catching her eye—they would probably walk on eggshells around each other for a while—Alice knew they'd be okay. Their friendship was strong and it could recover from this blow.

Yet a suffocating pain still lingered in Alice's chest; the hole there wasn't healing. Making peace with Madison had not been enough. Her heart was still shattered. Her friendship with Jack was over. For the first time in her life, Alice found herself preferring no-Jack to my-friend-Jack, and that, she feared, would not change.

***

As they worked on restoring the wardrobe as a team, Madison's phone started ringing. She dropped the dress she was carrying to take the phone out of her pocket. "It's Vicky, my likable cousin," she said. "I'd better pick up; she never calls unless it's important." Madison swiped a finger on her phone and paced around the room as she talked.

With the chain of work interrupted, they all paused to listen to the phone call.

"Hi, Vicky, what's up?" Madison asked.

Pause.

"Yeah, I'm okay. I had a bit of a rough day." Madison threw an apologetic glance at Alice, and Alice made an effort to smile. She couldn't believe that less than an hour ago she'd been ready to toss her friendship with Madison into the garbage.

"She's *what?* For real? How?" Madison fired questions at the phone. "You're not joking?" She sounded incredulous. "When? So soon? All right, you too. Love you." Madison hung up and turned to Alice. "You're never going to believe this!"

"What?" Alice asked, wary. She'd had enough surprises today.

"Georgiana is pregnant, and she's getting married to Tyler."

Alice was too shocked to speak.

Haley frowned. "Isn't she in grad school?"

"Yeah."

"Were they trying for a baby?" Haley asked, the hint of an accusation in her voice.

Madison smiled. "Vicky wouldn't give me specifics, but I have a suspicion there's more to the story than she let on..."

The possibility of a trick pregnancy was enough to leave Alice, Madison, and Haley gossiping and laughing together, the tension of the morning finally gone.

Thirty-six
Alice

Alice and Madison received the invitations to Georgiana's wedding on the same day. Haley wasn't invited to the wedding as she didn't know Georgiana well; she'd only ever seen her in freshman year at sorority meetings. The letters arrived as all three roommates were chilling in their living room. Madison and Alice opened the heavy cream envelopes while sitting side-by-side on the couch. The wedding would be in two weeks' time.

Madison broke the silence first. "It seems my pregnant cousin is having a shotgun wedding before her bump starts showing."

Since their argument, Madison had been quiet and subdued. But in the last few days, it had gotten worse. Her face had become paler, the bags under her eyes more pronounced. Alice couldn't remember the last time she'd seen Madison smile. Still, she had not asked. They were being perfectly normal with each other, but some sore feelings lingered.

"I still can't believe she's having a baby," Alice said, turning the card in her hands.

Georgiana had called Alice to deliver the happy news right after Madison had spoken with Vicky. Later, Madison had integrated the information with what she'd heard through her family's grape vine. The gossip was that Georgiana had deliberately stopped taking the pill to get herself accidentally-on-purpose pregnant.

"It's a pretty obvious consequence when you go off the pill," Madison said flatly.

"Are you sure that's true?" Alice didn't want to believe her mentor would sink so low to keep a man. Georgiana was smart, beautiful, and, to the outside world, the incarnation of confidence. "You think there's no chance it was one of those rare cases where the pill actually didn't work?"

"What?" Madison snorted. "That famous zero point one percent?"

"It could be," Alice insisted.

"No, it couldn't." Madison shook her head. "Georgiana did it on purpose."

"I agree with Mad here," Haley butted into the conversation, still tapping on her iPad. "The pill not working is the most overused excuse for getting pregnant by *accident*."

"Why would she do that?" Alice asked.

"To force the poor guy to marry her," Madison said.

"Yes, but why?"

Madison shrugged. "Because she wanted to marry him? I don't know."

Alice changed the subject. "So you're going to be a bridesmaid?"

"Unfortunately."

"Isn't it a good thing? Maybe she wants to reconnect with you."

"It's not a good thing, it's family politics," Madison said, sounding sure. "I'm her cousin, so I get a spot on the bridesmaids' roster. Tomorrow I have to go to a bridal shop and stomach Georgiana parading around in white gowns. I'm dreading her choice of bridesmaid outfits."

Alice was surprised. Weddings were Madison's thing; she was a hopeless romantic and loved them. But today, she sounded bitter. Even if this was Georgiana's wedding, why was her friend being so cynical and negative about everything?

"Oh, come on. If there's one thing you can't say about Georgiana, it's that she doesn't have a sense of style," Alice said. "She'd never pick ugly dresses, it'd ruin her ceremony."

"I hope you're right."

"You want to go together that day, or do you have special bridesmaid duties?" Alice asked.

"No. We should go together from here." Madison blushed.

Why the blush? Maybe she wanted to bring a date. Alice checked her invitation; it said plus one. "I mean, if you want to go with David—"

"No!" Madison said, too quickly. "Why would I want to go with him? We're not even dating anymore."

Haley perked up on the couch and, while Madison wasn't looking, they exchanged a completely silent conversation made of shrugs, wide eyes, and mouthed words: *"Did you know?" … "No, you?" … "No. What do you make of it?" … "No idea." … "If he hurt her, I'm going to kill him." … "I'll help."*

"Mad, are you okay?" Haley asked.

Madison shrugged. "Sure." She turned around with a fake smile plastered on her face. "So, the wedding." Madison's tone was upbeat and her change of subject so abrupt, Haley and Alice exchanged another we'll-get-to-the-bottom-of-this-later look. "I have to be there early to get my hair and makeup done by a professional. My dear cousin doesn't trust my grooming skills. I bet you can get special grooming privileges, too."

"You think?" Alice was skeptical although not about getting free hair and makeup.

"Yes. Unless…" Madison paused.

"What?" Alice asked.

"Are you sure *you* don't want to bring a date to the wedding?"

"One-hundred percent."

"Are you still avoiding Jack?"

"Yes."

"Why?"

"I'm too ashamed." Alice forgot Madison's troubles and concentrated on her own. "I told him I loved him. Worse, I told him that I've been carrying a torch for him since freshman year. I also yelled about being jealous of all his girlfriends. I can't stomach the idea of facing him after all that."

"Is he still calling you every day?" Haley asked. "He's called me only twice this week."

Jack had been harassing Haley—the neutral party in all this—almost as much as he had Alice.

"Yes," Alice confirmed. "Less often, though. We're down to two missed calls per day."

"Don't you want to know what he has to say?" Haley asked.

"Yes and no," Alice confessed.

"Why not?" Madison.

"I can't take what I said to him back this time, Madison. I can't pretend I was acting out because I was on the rebound from Ethan. Saying I love you, I've been in love with you for three years, is pretty final. We can't go back to being friends, it'd kill me. It's goodbye for good this time. I'm not ready."

"What if he has something different to say?" Haley asked.

"Like what? That he's finally realized he loves me, too? This is not a fairytale, and Jack is no Prince Charming."

Alice stood up from the couch and braced her hands on the window frame. Whenever she rehearsed her angry declaration to Jack in her head, her face burned with shame. *I'm in love with you... I have been since freshman year... I had to watch you go through girl after girl... I hated every single one... I was jealous... I spent years hoping one day you'd notice me...*

The humiliation was too much.

"When he came here searching for you," Madison said cautiously, "he didn't look like a worried friend."

Alice stiffened. She didn't want to discuss Jack with Madison; the wound was still too fresh. "What did he look like, then?" she asked.

"To be honest, like a crazed lover. He punched the wall."

Instinctively, Alice turned to stare at the wall and found her roommates staring, too. "Yeah, right."

"I'm being serious," Madison insisted.

"I saw him, too," Haley said. "He looked desperate."

"Did he say anything specific?"

"No, but—" Madison started.

"No, exactly," Alice snapped. "Can we drop the topic now?"

"What would you like to talk about?" Madison asked. "I've got no love life to complain about."

"So you ended it for good with David?" Haley asked.

"Yes." Madison winced. "Better no love life than a crappy one."

"What—" Haley started.

"I don't want to talk about it," Madison hissed.

"Are we doing a bachelorette?" Alice changed the subject completely. It was clear whatever had happened between Madison and David was still too raw.

"No," Madison said. "Since Georgiana's pregnant, we'll do a bridal/baby shower two-in-one."

"When?" Alice asked.

"Next weekend."

"Okay, so we have the shower next week, and the wedding the week after?"

"Correct," Madison confirmed. "And tomorrow is shopping with Bridezilla, but that's just for *lucky* me."

"What am I going to do alone for two weekends?" Haley asked.

"Want to swap lives?" Madison asked. "What do we need? A shooting star, or something? Find me the star, and I'll make the wish in a heartbeat."

Haley rolled her eyes. "Your family can't be that bad." She turned to Alice for confirmation. "Right?"

Alice took Madison's side. "The Smithsons can be overbearing at times."

"The voice of truth." Madison made a thank-you gesture and sighed. "I hope three weekends in a row with my family won't send me to therapy."

***

The next weekend, Alice followed Madison up the front steps of her aunt and uncle's massive townhouse for the bachelorette/baby shower. Madison stopped on the doorstep, visibly reluctant to go in. Alice stepped forward and rang the bell.

Georgiana opened the door. "Alice! I still can't get over the hair, so fabulous." Georgiana hugged her and then switched her attention to Madison. "Madison," she said with a tight-lipped smile. "You might want to try a blowout sometimes; I hear it does wonders for unruly curls. Come on in, everyone's outside."

Madison rolled her eyes, then took Alice's arm under hers and guided her through the house toward the backyard. Okay, Alice thought, so Georgiana really was a bit bitchy with Madison.

The setting outside was stylish in an overwhelming, pastel-colors way. Pastel decorations, pastel gazebo, pastel food, and pastel-wrapped presents. Pastel pink seemed to be the dominant color.

"Is she having a girl?" Alice asked.

"I think it's too soon to say," Madison said.

"There's a lot of pink here."

"Eh, you know Georgiana." Madison shrugged. "She probably thinks she can influence the sex of the baby by sheer willpower."

Alice looked down at the bright, rainbow-patterned present in her hands. "Let's go drop this off."

They walked toward a table piled with presents, and she deposited hers on top. It clashed so badly with the harmonious pastel theme that Alice immediately removed it from the top and hid it at the back.

"Where's yours?" Alice asked.

"No idea. My mom was in charge of the presents from our side of the family. Probably something expensive," Madison added, her voice tainted by jealousy. "It's not like I'm going to spend my own money on my bitch cousin."

"How about your unborn niece?"

"Or nephew," Madison pointed out. "Let's see how he/she turns out first. Hey, why don't we go say hello to my mom?" Madison pointed at a stylish woman in the distance and steered Alice that way.

Alice loved Madison's mom. Of all her friend's relatives, she was the most easygoing and probably the one who'd passed on to Madison her boho style. Alice suspected it had a lot to do with the fact that Madison's mom had not been a Smithson from birth.

"Did you pick the bridesmaid dress?" Alice asked as they walked.

"No, *she* did."

"What color?"

"*Pastel* lavender," Madison said mockingly.

Alice suppressed a laugh. "Is it bad?"

"No, you were right," Madison conceded. "She's too stylish to pick a hideous dress. Hi, Mom…"

They chatted with Madison's mom until Mrs. Smithson was called away to solve a catering problem, and then they headed back to the buffet.

Alice was trying to decide what to eat when Georgiana waltzed over and grabbed a light-blue pastry. "Alice," she said. "Try these azure ones, they're delicious. Madison," Georgiana continued. "You might want to stick to the white pastries, they're sugar-free. You know, in case you're watching your weight."

Alice half-choked on a bite of her "azure" tart. Georgiana definitely was snarky with Madison in a way she'd never seen her be with anyone else.

A loud crash resounded in the background, and they all turned in the direction of the noise. A server had tripped and dropped an entire tray of glasses.

"Those idiots," Georgiana snapped. "Ladies, excuse me; I have to go make sure this party doesn't get ruined by substandard house help."

Alice smiled awkwardly and, out of the corner of her eye, caught Madison throwing away the cake pop she'd only half eaten.

Alice could pretend not to have seen, but she felt the need to say something. "You know you can eat the whole tray if you want. You don't have any weight issues."

"No." Madison sighed, that air of lingering, unexplained sorrow crossing her eyes. "She made me get my dress half a size smaller than my usual. So she's right, I need to watch what I eat."

"No, you really don't." Alice picked up another azure tart and pushed it into Madison's hand. "Eat this, it's really delicious."

Madison grabbed it and bit half off, smiling. "Mmm, you're right… these are divine."

Alice wished everything in life could be solved with a blue—sorry, *azure*—tart.

***

The day of the wedding, Madison and Alice left their apartment to drive together to the Smithson's country house in Madison's car. Madison was wearing her lilac, one-shoulder strap bridesmaid gown, and Alice was in a simple blush cocktail dress. Alice had not dared wear anything that wasn't pastel. They'd left their hair loose and wore no makeup, as per wedding planner-issued instructions. A professional would take care of them before the ceremony started.

At the house, the whole pampering process was extremely efficient. A stern-looking wedding planner ushered them to a small room to change into black silk kimonos and then moved them into different rooms, one for each beauty task: hair, makeup, nails, and a final station where they got back their (steamed) dresses. The wedding planner and her assistants kept muttering, "Divide and conquer."

Throughout the entire process, Alice was alone. She never caught a glimpse of the bride or Madison until she was ushered back into a changing room and found her roommate already there. Madison, who usually never wore makeup, looked stunning in her gown with her golden locks arranged in a complicated chignon. When Alice was dressed, too, a scary assistant ordered them to go wait inside the church, which was even-in-heels-walking distance.

The first guests had already started to arrive and Ethan was helping his father welcome everyone. Many voices were overlapping, the typical Boston accent mixing with a southern lilt. The groom was originally from Texas. Alice shuffled through the entrance door with Madison at her heels, trying to avoid catching Ethan's gaze; she hadn't seen her ex since their breakup.

For now, Madison sat with Alice on the bride's side of the church, halfway to the back. Yet, soon, she would have to go backstage to make her official entrance as the ceremony began.

"Is the best man a woman?" Alice asked, squinting her eyes.

"Yep, Rose," Madison confirmed. "Ethan's girlfriend."

"You're right!" Alice exclaimed. "I didn't recognize her primped like that; if it wasn't for the chignon, you could take her for a guy."

"Yeah, Georgiana forbid her from wearing a dress or doing her hair in any style other than a low chignon."

"Seriously? Why?"

Madison shrugged. "I guess she wanted to make sure no one stole her thunder. As if." She snorted.

Rose was talking to the minister. Alice felt weird watching her; it was like spying, in a way. Maybe it was normal to be fascinated by the woman your ex-boyfriend had chosen over you. The visual stalking of her old rival didn't last long. Rose soon finished her conversation and vanished through a door on the right of the altar, presumably where the groom was waiting.

At that moment, Ethan walked past them and disappeared behind the same door as Rose. He didn't recognize Alice, or he pretended not to. After five minutes, he came back out and nodded to the priest. The groom and best woman followed and took their spots at the altar.

"I have to go," Madison said. "I'll catch up with you later." And she was gone.

The wedding march started playing a few minutes later as the bridesmaids and bride made their way down the aisle. The minister started talking and before Alice knew it, the ceremony was over. *It doesn't take long to change your life forever.* She tried to wait for Madison to walk back to the house, but her friend was in the thick of the crowd with the rest of the family so Alice decided to fly solo.

At the house, the reception was taking place in the gardens. Waiters were already passing out champagne flutes and some aperitifs, so Alice grabbed a flute of the bubbly. She removed her shoes to walk on the grass, feeling strangely isolated amidst the crowd of guests. Weddings did weird things to a girl's emotions.

Alice's mood didn't improve during lunch. She didn't know anyone at her table, which was obviously the singles table—seven women and a grand total of three guys sat around her. A perfect reproduction of the dating men-women split. For Alice, it was an effort to sustain polite conversations for the three hours the five-course meal required. So, when the dessert buffet was announced, Alice seized the opportunity immediately and shot out of her chair to stretch her legs.

Thirty-seven

Rose

Rose left Ethan at their table and strolled around the dessert buffet. She took a plate and piled it with all sorts of treats. As she reached the chocolate bonbons, Rose noticed a pretty girl throw her a furtive glance and then lower her gaze just as quickly.

The girl's face looked familiar, but... *different* was the word. As if something was not quite as it should be.

"Hi," Rose said, unable to keep her curiosity in check. "Have we met before?"

The girl gaped at Rose, eyes wide with... surprise? Fear? It couldn't be fear. Who would be afraid of Rose, and why?

"Just the once," the girl said, her tone not exactly warm. "I was a blonde when we last met, though."

Rose tried to mentally Photoshop the girl's long dark strands into golden ones, seeing if she could guess where they had met.

The girl cut her memory exercise short by saying, "I'm Alice." She paused. "Ethan's ex."

Rose couldn't help blushing. The image of a pretty blonde girl staring daggers at her the night she'd met Ethan popped into her mind's eye. He was dating Alice at the time and had broken up with her to start dating Rose.

Alice was more striking as a brunette; the new hairstyle made her appear more mature.

"Alice, sure. I'm Rose. I don't believe we were properly introduced before." She offered her hand, hoping Ethan's ex didn't hold too much of a grudge. After all, it had happened almost a year ago.

Alice seemed to consider for a second before taking her hand. "Nice to meet you," she said, and quickly let go. The ex piled more chocolates on her plate and took a step backward. "I have to go back to my table. It was nice seeing you again."

"Yeah, sure."

Rose watched Alice run away, then made her way back to her own table. Ethan was gone, so she sat down to enjoy her mini desserts. While she was eating, the band started playing and people all around her stood up to dance.

"Miss Atwood," Ethan said, appearing next to her. "May I have the honor of a dance?" He bent forward in a hint of a bow and offered his hand.

Rose let go of the chocolate pastry she was holding. Ethan was so much better than chocolate. She marveled once again at how much she loved him. Especially when he played the gallant, gentleman hero.

She took his hand, smiling. "Most certainly, Mr. Smithson."

Ethan led her onto the dance floor. They'd never danced together, not this formally, at least. But they were doing a great job of it all the same.

"Where did you learn to dance?" he asked.

"I had to partake in the renowned Dallas Symphony Orchestra League Presentation Ball for debutantes," Rose said jokingly. "What about you? I didn't know you could dance so well." She was honestly surprised—he was leading her like a professional.

Ethan's jaw tensed slightly. "Sabrina made me take lessons when we were engaged."

"Oh, I'm sorry." Rose was horrified.

"Don't be." Ethan smiled his most dashing smile, making the corners of his eyes go all crinkly and igniting a sparkle in them. "At least something good came out of that engagement." He squeezed her hand.

Rose squeezed it back. It was the first time he'd spoken about Sabrina in a lighthearted way. Rose liked to take credit for this newfound easiness about his past.

"Speaking of exes… did you know Alice is here?"

"I haven't seen her, but it figures." Ethan spun Rose away and made her pirouette back. "Alice is Georgiana's young sister or little sister; I never understood sorority tiers very well."

"She's dyed her hair. She looks good," Rose said provocatively, prodding Ethan's feelings for his ex.

"You look good." Ethan pulled her closer. "I'm not sure if the fact that I find you hot while you're dressed like a boy should scare me or not," Ethan teased as he and Rose waltzed across the dance floor—a platform that had been set up in the middle of the Smithson's family home garden.

"I'm about to cut into your dilemma," Rose said. "Do you think the style-gestapo will flay me if I let my hair loose? This chignon is killing me. And the bow tie is strangling! How do you guys wear these around your neck every day?" She started pulling some pins out of her hair.

"Here, let me help…" Ethan pulled her to the edge of the garden and started working his fingers through her hair.

When the last pin came loose, Rose shook her head and let her hair cascade down onto her shoulders. Ethan was already undoing the bow tie.

"I have to stop now, or I'll end up undressing you completely. It wouldn't be very proper."

"No, it wouldn't, especially not with your mother staring at us. She's been watching us like a hawk all day. What's up with her?"

"Ah, my dear." Ethan grinned. "I'm afraid that with my sister's nuptials, I remain the sole Smithson sibling yet to be matched. I'm pretty sure my mother has designs on you."

"Aren't two weddings in six months enough for her?"

"Is the thought of joining yourself to me in holy matrimony so unappealing to you, Miss Atwood?"

"What? No, I-I mean…" Rose was stuttering, her face searing red. "Are you serious?"

"Why not?"

His stare was like burning ice.

"I thought you w-were against getting married."

"I'm against girls shopping for rings after one date. I'm not against getting married to the woman I love."

"Are you proposing?" Rose's heart was beating way too fast.

"Now, don't go getting a big head, Miss Atwood…"

She swatted him playfully. "Jerk."

He grabbed her hand and pulled her into a kiss.

"I love you," Ethan whispered. "One day, I want you to be my wife. What do you say?"

"One day." Rose couldn't help but smile like an idiot. "I love you, too."

"Now that my noble intentions are in the open, can I bring you to my room?"

Ethan and Rose discreetly disappeared behind a bush and ran across the lawn toward the house, holding hands and laughing like a pair of kids.

***

The inside of Ethan's house was so stylish it was scary. It was an impeccable mix of rustic and modern design, a balance hard to get right. From tiny objects to each major furnishing element, everything was placed perfectly. Nothing left to chance. It was impressive but somehow made the place feel more like a museum than a lived-in home. All this flawlessness could get suffocating. Rose felt for Ethan. Being a Smithson really came with a lot of pressure attached. *Imagine being an unruly kid in this house.*

Rose followed Ethan up the stairs and through a corridor with too many white doors to count. He stopped in front of one toward the end, pausing with his hand on the handle. "You're about to have a glimpse into my teenage lifestyle." He flung the door open and a loud snore came from within.

Sprawled on Ethan's bed was a bulging, middle-aged man, fast asleep.

"Rose, meet Uncle Frank." Ethan sighed. "He must've decided my room was as good a place as any to fall asleep."

Rose giggled, taking in what she could of Ethan's room before he closed the door. She took inventory of his life when he was younger. Items of an over-achiever: awards, certificates, sports trophies. But also a cool, popular kid: a rock band poster, shots of him posing with his friends and lacrosse teammates. His smile was already irresistible, even back then. Then there were the obligatory family photos, stored in elegant frames his mother must have bought. They showed his well-adjusted side: his parents, Ethan with his sisters, and a photo of the entire Smithson clan.

The door clicked shut, and they tiptoed away, careful not to wake the sleeping man.

"We'll have to take one of the guest rooms." Ethan turned on his heel and headed back toward the beginning of the hall.

He opened a random door. Before Rose could peek inside, Ethan roared and rushed into the room. Rose made to follow him but stopped dead on the threshold. She raised a hand to cover her mouth as she stared at the scene before her eyes in shocked silence.

Ethan was holding Tyler against the wall by the neck of his unbuttoned shirt. On the rumpled bed lay a cowering girl, her eyes big with fear. Rose took in her wrinkled bridesmaid dress, messed up hair, and kissed-away lipstick, and the reality of what had happened here hit her in the stomach.

"I'm going to kill you, you bastard," Ethan hissed in cold rage. He drew his elbow back, closing his hand into a tight fist, and cranking his arm back to punch Tyler in the face.

Rose jumped forward and took a hold of her boyfriend's arm before he could land the blow. "Ethan, stop!" she yelled.

"What?" He turned toward her, glowering, his eyes crazed. "Are you going to defend him, even now?"

"No, no," Rose hurried to say. "But think: you can't reduce his face to a pulp without having to explain what's going on to everyone downstairs. That would be even worse for Georgiana."

For a split second, Ethan seemed not to care what anyone would say. But he took a deep, steadying breath and lowered his arm without hitting Tyler. Instead, he yanked Tyler off his feet and hurled him across the room, sending him crashing against a wooden dressing table. The dresser capsized and Tyler careened to the floor.

"What are you guys doing?" Vicky, Ethan's other sister, stepped into the room. "I could hear the noise from downstairs." She took in the scene and closed the door behind her before demanding again, "What's going on here?"

Where Ethan's rage was intense and outspoken, Vicky's was calm and controlled, but no less brutal. Her blue eyes, the same color as Ethan's, were cold and smoldering at the same time.

Ethan was leaning against the wall, looking exhausted. He made an I-can't-talk gesture and shook his head.

Vicky turned to the girl on the bed next, who said, "I'm sorry" and began to sob.

Rose was the only one cool enough to speak. "We came into the room and found them on the bed. Tyler must be drunk."

She threw a reproachful look at her best friend. Tyler was sitting on the floor with his elbows resting on his bent knees and his face hidden in his hands.

Vicky's cold fury turned toward the bridesmaid first. "Madison, I know you've always had it in for Georgiana, but this?" She waved a hand between the girl and Tyler. "On her wedding day?"

"I'm s-sorry," the girl whimpered.

"She's your cousin!" Vicky barked. "We're family, for goodness' sake."

"P-please don't tell my parents." The girl's eyes seemed to become wider still.

Vicky seemed about to spit a gruff retort, but instead, she took a deep breath and started pacing in circles, staring at the floor and holding her chin in one hand. She stopped and said, "We're not going to tell anyone." The middle Smithson sibling took turns staring down everyone present. "What happened here today doesn't leave this room."

"Are you kidding me?" Ethan raged. "Our sister married this scum bag, who couldn't be faithful to her for half a day. Gigi has a right to know; she could get an annulment or something."

"Our sister isn't going to want an annulment," Vicky said.

"Not even after this?"

"I don't think so." Vicky shook her head. "Georgiana is too stubborn to admit she was wrong, and she's still pregnant with his baby."

Rose heart broke a little as she watched pain and anger mix on Ethan's face. "It doesn't mean they have to stay married," he said, "not if this is how it's going to be."

"Ethan." Vicky was not backing down. "I'm sorry to break it you, but as much as I love her, our sister lied to him about being on the pill. She maneuvered to get herself pregnant. Georgiana forced this on him, knowing what she was doing all along."

Rose agreed with everything Vicky was saying, and she was glad that for once she wasn't the one who had to tell Ethan. Whenever Rose tried to point out that this was a two-person mess, and that Georgiana wasn't exactly an innocent victim, Ethan left on the jealousy wagon, making it all about her history with Tyler. He'd never forgiven Rose for not allowing him to tell Georgiana that Tyler had cheated on her with Rose. Ethan was convinced Georgiana would not be pregnant now if she had known. Rose wasn't so sure, and to have someone else reason with him was a welcome novelty. They'd already had too many arguments about Tyler and, frankly, defending her best friend was getting harder and harder. Rose was ashamed of him, and also of the tiny part of herself that was relieved it wasn't her that had married Tyler.

Rose stared up at Ethan, the man she loved with all her heart, the man who'd saved her, and she wished she had a way to comfort him. He looked so anguished.

"Well," Ethan said, then took his rage out on the ottoman at the base of the bed with a violent kick. "No one forced him to propose or to cheat on our sister on their wedding day!"

The statement seemed to give Vicky pause. She crouched on the floor next to Tyler. "You. Hey, you!" She snapped her fingers in his face. "Look at me."

Tyler slowly lifted his head.

"What happened here?"

Thirty-eight
Tyler

"I freaked out," Tyler said, barely able to focus on Georgiana's sister crouched next to him. "People kept telling me all these marriage and new-daddy jokes, and I just started downing one drink after the other, and I lost it..." What a pathetic excuse. He was pathetic. If he couldn't keep it together for a few hours, how was he going to manage a lifetime? "I don't know what I'm doing."

"Fair enough. Listen." Vicky paused until Tyler's eyes focused on hers. "I know you didn't ask to be a father, but you're going to become one, anyway. As our nephew or niece's dad, you're part of the family now no matter what." Vicky was talking in a calm, polite voice that surprised Tyler. "Now, you can be a good father even if you're not married to our sister," Vicky continued. "Was this a last minute case of cold feet, or is it how you plan to behave from now on?"

Tyler's pulse raced. What did he want? He wanted to be a good dad, and for his child to grow up with two parents. So what was he doing here?

"Th-this is not..." he stuttered. "It wasn't... I want to try."

"Okay. You get this one pass." Vicky raised one finger eye-level between them. "And that's it."

Ethan emitted a disbelieving grunt from his corner. Tyler didn't dare look at him. Of all the people in the world, why did it have to be he and Rose who had walked in on him? *Still better than my pregnant wife,* Tyler thought. The weight of what he had almost done to his wife made him sick. What if Ethan and Rose hadn't been here? Would he have had sex with Georgiana's cousin? *Probably, yes.* What the hell was wrong with him?

Vicky stood up. "Go wash your face and pull yourself together." She offered him a hand and helped him up off the floor.

Tyler did as he was told and disappeared into the en-suite bathroom. He didn't dare meet anyone's eye, particularly not Rose's. In one look, he'd be able to read all her thoughts, and he couldn't cope with the reproach and disappointment he was bound to find written in her dark eyes. Tyler gently closed the door behind himself and braced his arms on either side of the sink. He stared in the mirror.

Someone he didn't like stared back. Georgiana wasn't perfect, but she didn't deserve this. More than everything, his unborn child did not deserve to come into the world in a broken family. He'd been stupid and weak. Tyler shook his head. How had this whole mess even started?

During the banquet, Tyler remembered shuffling around the tables alongside Georgiana. She'd made him take turns greeting all the guests. His relatives, her relatives, friends from Boston, friends from Texas, there had been so many. Every group ready to offer advice or words of wisdom. Tyler had smiled and endured it. They had drunk a toast at each table—well, Georgiana hadn't, she was sticking to virgin mimosas—but Tyler had downed one glass of champagne after the other. He'd needed the alcohol to endure jab after jab about married life, newborns, and shrinking bank accounts. His anxiety had grown with every new joke. He had another year left in school, and yet he was already expected to provide for a wife and a child. Tyler came from a wealthy family, as did Georgiana, so money wasn't a problem—in theory. Provided he kept asking his parents for support. With Georgiana's expensive tastes, he couldn't buy a bigger home, repay student loans, and sustain a family without economic help from his parents. So that was his independence flying out the window, and it *sucked.*

When the meal finally ended, Tyler had left his table with the excuse of needing some air. He had gone to hide behind a tall hedge that shielded him from view. The girl, Madison, Georgiana's cousin—he hadn't known she was her cousin at the time—was there hiding, too. They'd started talking, then he'd asked her if there was a place he could wash his face. She'd shown him to the downstairs bathroom, but there was a line so they'd gone upstairs. Madison said he could use one of the guest rooms, and before he knew what was happening, they were kissing on the bed instead. He was cheating on his wife three hours after they got married.

Never again.

He'd be a father soon. It didn't matter if Georgiana had tricked him, that he hadn't asked for this, and that he was scared as hell. He already loved this child with all his heart; nothing else mattered.

Tyler stared hard at himself, vowing not to be the kind of d-bag who cheated on his wife. Turning on the tap, he splashed cold water on his face. This had been his wake-up call. Vicky was right—the situation sucked. But since he had decided to marry Georgiana, he had to give the marriage a fair shot.

Tyler finished washing his face then straightened his spine, his jaw set with determination. He buttoned his shirt, adjusted his cuffs, and re-did the knot of his bowtie until it looked impeccable. There, the image of the perfect groom. One pass, Vicky had said. That's all he needed; he would not screw up again.

Thirty-nine

Rose

After sending Tyler to get it together in the en suite, Vicky turned toward her cousin, who was still sobbing on the bed. "Did you come here in your car?" she asked. "Can you go home right away?"

"I drove here, but I came with my roommate."

"Your roommate?" Vicky seemed surprised. "What's her name? How come she was invited?"

"Alice. You met her," the girl said.

Is it possible the roommate is Ethan's Alice? Small world, Rose thought. A furtive glance at Ethan confirmed that, yes, it was the same Alice.

"Alice is Georgiana's friend, too," the disgraced bridesmaid continued. "She came to our house for Christmas the year before last, and she was at the baby shower. We were talking about her on Martha's Vineyard, remember?"

"I was getting married I don't remember anything anyone said to me that week, but I remember her from Christmas…" Vicky stared at the ceiling pensively. "A cute blonde, right? I didn't see her in the crowd today or at the shower."

"She's a brunette now."

"That explains it, then," Vicky said matter-of-factly. "It doesn't matter, anyway. You can't tell her about what happened here."

"Alice is my best friend," the girl protested. "She won't tell Georgiana."

"Madison, listen to me." Vicky closed the distance to the bed. "I'm not kidding. You can't tell anyone about this. Promise me."

The girl looked scared again. "Okay, I promise. I won't tell anyone."

"Can you ask your roommate if she can get a ride with someone else?"

On impulse, Rose said, "We can give her a lift."

Ethan arched his brows. "Are you sure?"

Rose nodded.

Noticing the underlying tension in Ethan's question, Vicky asked, "Why the face? You know her, too?"

"Alice and I dated a while ago," he explained.

"Seriously?"

Ethan shrugged.

"Ah well, that's taken care of. Madison, are you sure you're okay to drive? Did you drink?"

"No, not much."

That's a lie, Rose thought. From the state of her, Madison wasn't wasted, but she wasn't anywhere close to sober either.

"Are you sure?" Vicky echoed Rose's worries. "We can call a car if you're not okay."

"I'm good," the girl insisted. "I can drive."

"Okay."

Rose wasn't convinced, but Vicky was calling the shots and Rose didn't want to contradict her.

"Here." Ethan's sister handed their cousin a wet wipe. "Clean your face," she instructed.

Madison's mascara was running in rivulets down her flushed cheeks. She scrubbed her face with the tissue, making her skin even blotchier. Under all that melted makeup, the girl was stunning. Blue eyes, high cheekbones covered in cute freckles, and otherwise regular features that made her a classic beauty. Madison freed her hair from the half-undone, elaborate chignon all the bridesmaids had, letting loose a cascade of golden looks. Even more beautiful. Yet her face, for all its beauty, was twisted ugly with remorse, shame, and a mix of other complicated emotions Rose couldn't discern.

Vicky waited for her to be finished cleaning herself before she spoke again. "Do you know how to get out of the house from the back?"

"Yes." Madison nodded.

"Okay. I'll call you tonight and we'll talk this through. But not a word to anyone else."

Madison grabbed her clutch from the bedside table and fled the room. Watching her run, Rose couldn't help the gush of pity in her chest.

"Ethan." Vicky turned her attention on him next. Solving one problem at a time, snap-snap-snap. "Can you please go grab an aspirin and some water?"

"Yeah." Ethan threw a murderous stare at the bathroom where Tyler was still holed up. "It's better if I get out of here." He exited the bedroom.

"Will Madison be all right?" Rose asked.

"What makes you ask that?"

"She seemed really…" Rose paused to find the right word. "Broken."

Vicky hugged herself. "Madison has always harbored a major inferiority complex toward me, and toward Georgiana especially. And everyone else, really: her friends, the girls in her sorority, you name it. My sister didn't help cure any of her insecurities either. You know how she can be."

Rose was surprised to hear Vicky hint again that Georgiana was far from perfect. She knew the two sisters were close, and she'd assumed it meant they were alike. In reality, they couldn't have been more different.

Vicky kept going. "And my whole family is so damn competitive that growing up a shy, reserved kid… Madison hasn't had an easy time of it. Don't worry, I'll call her later and talk with her. Really talk. I'm not going to point the finger. Ethan has never understood the female pecking order of this family, but I do, and I'm sorry to say Madison has been at the bottom her entire life."

The more Vicky talked, the more Rose liked her. "At least she can count on you," she said.

"Madison is like another younger sister." Vicky braced her hands on the bed's footboard. "I can at least try to understand the perverse train of thought that brought her to behave like she has today. After years of being bullied by Georgiana, she probably saw this as retribution."

"Bullied?"

"Bullied is too strong a word." Ethan's sister waved a hand. "Outshined, teased. Let's say Georgiana usually wins the competition to get the most attention at the dinner table. Madison is fragile. She doesn't know how to stand up for herself. So she probably decided to backstab

Georgiana, get the other end of the stick for once. It makes me sick to my stomach that my family is so messed up."

"It's not," Rose said.

Vicky raised a skeptical eyebrow.

"Well, maybe a little," Rose conceded. "But the important thing is that you stick together no matter what."

"I hope you're right. What about your friend in there?" Vicky pointed to the still-closed bathroom door. "Do you think Tyler will be capable of keeping his word, or do I have to send home all the bridesmaids?"

Rose considered the question for a few seconds. "Usually, he's on his best behavior for a while after he's messed up. Especially with something as big as this. I know he wants to try, but he probably feels trapped by so many responsibilities he didn't ask for." Rose shrugged. "I'm sure he will be a great father and he will *try* to be a good husband."

"It's more than I would've done in his place."

"Really?"

"Yeah. I love my sister," Vicky said fiercely, "in the same way you love your cat after he's peed on your favorite rug. The way she tricked Tyler into becoming a father is inexcusable. No matter how you look at it."

"Still, Georgiana doesn't deserve this." Rose stared at the crumpled bed sheets.

Vicky gave her a long stare. "That's kind of you. I know you two have your own history and don't like each other much."

"Yeah… we… uh…" Rose didn't know what to say.

"But I do like you," Vicky added. "I want you to know that. I've never seen my brother this happy."

Rose was taken aback. Vicky was proving to be one of the coolest people she'd ever met. Rose smiled and nodded. "I like you too."

Ethan came back into the room with a bottle of spring water and a plastic vial of aspirin tablets. "What are you two smiling about?" he asked gloomily.

"Nothing," they both answered.

Ethan passed the water and tablets to his sister.

"Thanks," she said. "You two go. I'll stay with the groom until he's good enough to come back out."

Ethan gave his sister a stiff nod and moved outside the room. Rose smiled at Vicky one last time and then followed him. He was already headed for the stairs.

"Hey, come here." Rose grabbed his hand to stop him and hugged him.

"Please." Ethan tried to push her back, but she wouldn't let him. "Don't even try to defend him."

"I wasn't going to." She took Ethan's face in her hands. "I want to know how *you* feel."

Ethan's jaw relaxed, and he stopped struggling to get away. "I can handle it."

"Are you sure?"

"Yeah, I have you." He finally placed his arms around her waist. "I'm good."

Rose kissed him. "I love you."

"I love you, too. Now, let's go before people start wondering where everyone went."

"Right." Rose smirked. "And we have to tell Alice she just earned herself an awkward ride home."

Forty

Alice

Alice spotted Rose and Ethan coming out of the house. She had to admit they were a beautiful couple. After everything that had happened with Jack and Peter in the past year, Ethan was ancient history. But still, seeing your ex and his new perfect girlfriend so in love wasn't exactly ideal.

They seemed to be walking in her direction, so Alice turned her back to them and grabbed a flute of champagne from a passing waiter. Surely they would try to avoid her just as much as she was trying to avoid them. The last thing Alice expected when she turned back was to find them standing right behind her as if they wanted to speak to her. She almost choked on her drink and recovered just in time to avoid making a complete fool of herself.

"Hi, Alice," Ethan said. Rose smiled apologetically.

"Hi," Alice replied warily.

"Madison wasn't feeling well," Ethan said. "She had to go home and asked me to tell you."

Alice had seen Madison drink more than one glass of wine. Should she even be driving? "Is she sick?" Alice asked, the embarrassment of facing her ex replaced by worry for her friend. "What did she have?"

"Nothing serious. She was just a bit lightheaded."

Ethan's jaw kept twitching as he spoke. That added to the way Rose was shifting uncomfortably from one foot to the other, and Alice was positive they weren't telling her the whole story.

Alice dropped her glass on a nearby table and reached into her clutch for her phone. She had one new text from Madison.

Not feeling well, heading home

Alice scrolled through the chat, but there were no other messages. Things didn't add up. She lifted her head and asked, "Is Madison gone already?"

"Should be." Ethan shrugged.

His hostile attitude was pushing Alice's buttons. Was he mad at Madison? Because she wasn't feeling well? "So you let her drive home alone when she was feeling lightheaded?" Alice pressed him. That didn't sound much like Ethan; it didn't sound like any of the Smithson clan.

"It wasn't that serious."

"But serious enough she had to go home."

Alice wasn't sure why she was trying to pick a fight, especially with her ex. But she wanted to find out what it was that they weren't telling her.

"Anyway, Madison should have texted you to tell you," Ethan said, ignoring her question point blank. "Since she was your ride, we can give you a lift home."

A lift home with her ex and the girl he'd dumped her for? *Hell no!*

"Err." Alice put the phone back in her purse to gain a couple of seconds. She had to wiggle her way out of this situation. "Yeah, she did text me. Don't you worry, guys. I can call an Uber to get home."

"I live just off campus," Rose said. "It's not a problem

for us to drop you off. It'd cost you a fortune to get a car to come all the way here and back to Cambridge."

Ethan's girlfriend was being so genuinely kind and warm, it was impossible to say no. And Alice wasn't good at thinking on her feet. *Madison had better be seriously ill.*

"Okay, then," Alice sighed. "When do you guys want to go?"

"After they cut the cake?" Ethan looked at Rose who nodded.

"All right, that's settled," Alice said. "I'll see you later, guys." She walked away as quickly as she could without appearing to be running.

Not long afterward, the band stopped playing and the wedding planner took the stage to ask all the guests to group on the lawn for the cutting of the cake. They formed a big semicircle around a small round table covered with a white cloth. On top of it stood the wedding cake—a five-layer tower decorated with a waterfall of pale pink-and-white sugar flowers.

Alice waited to see where Ethan and Rose would go, and positioned herself on the opposite side, at the back of the crowd. When all the guests were settled, soft music started in the background and Georgiana and Tyler made their appearance from inside the house. The bride and groom crossed the garden holding hands, Georgiana looking positively radiant in her amazing high-low hem gown and Tyler appearing too pale for his own good. He was smiling, but something was off. His smile looked forced. Was he nervous?

As the bride and groom took their place behind the small table, Georgiana's older sister discretely emerged from the house. Victoria scanned the crowd, then joined

Ethan and Rose. They all started whispering furiously to one another, heads bent in a close circle. The argument seemed to become heated, so much so that Vicky made a "be quiet" gesture, peering over her shoulder. Alice's suspicions flared up again. It looked like the three of them were discussing some big secret the guests shouldn't overhear.

Ethan went quiet and fixed his gaze ahead. Rose was studying his face apprehensively. Why? Alice followed Ethan's stare: he was glaring at the groom with murder written all over his features. Alice had never seen him so livid. Vicky's mouth, too, was set in a thin line, and she sported a deep frown. Georgiana appeared to be the only unabashedly happy Smithson sibling. What was all the drama about?

A cheer erupted from the crowd as Georgiana and Tyler joined hands and sunk a knife into the cake's top layer. Alice drained her glass and walked back to her table to wait for a slice of the wedding cake as did most of the guests. She wasn't hungry; she'd had enough of the wedding banquet, and her stomach was knotting tighter and tighter at the prospect of her awkward ride home. But, apparently, it was bad luck to leave a wedding without having a bite of the cake. And she could use some good fortune.

The cake was too sweet, so after the first perfunctory bite, Alice left the rest. She was about to go search for Ethan and Rose when Georgiana appeared by her side.

"I'm throwing the bouquet," the bride announced, taking Alice's hand. "You have to come."

Alice followed her and joined the crowd of eager-looking—to say the least, belligerent to be more accurate—single girls ready to catch the prize. Around her, crazed women started pushing and shoving, so Alice decided to move to the edge of the swaying crowd.

"All right, ladies," Georgiana yelled, and winked at Alice. "Here it goes. One… two… three…"

The bouquet soared high in the air and almost hit Alice in the face before she caught it. A disappointed groan resounded around her. The bouquet felt heavier than she'd imagined. *Fat chance I'm getting married within the year,* she thought.

Georgiana barreled into her, yelling, "I knew you'd catch it!" The bride pulled her into a hug, the beading on her dress scraping Alice's skin at multiple points. "Thanks so much for coming. I'm sorry we didn't get to talk much today, but everyone wanted a piece of me."

"Of course." Alice smiled. "You're the most beautiful bride in the world."

"I have to go now." Georgiana was more hyper than a hamster on a wheel. "Tyler and I have to say our goodbyes before going."

"Are you leaving for the honeymoon tonight?" Alice asked.

"Yeah." Georgiana nodded. "We'd better hurry. I'll call you when I get back, all right?"

"Sure, have a great time."

They hugged again, and Georgiana waltzed away in a whirl of white organza. With no excuses left to delay the inevitable, Alice sighed and started searching for Ethan and Rose. It was Rose who found her instead.

"Alice, here," she called, pushing her way through the crowd to reach her. "We're ready to go if you are."

"Are you sure you wouldn't rather I took a cab?"

"This far out of the city? It'd be expensive," Rose said.

"Listen, I understand this might be awkward for you…"

"Well, a bit," Alice admitted. "Isn't it for you, too?"

"Honestly, I'm cool if you're cool. Ethan, too." Rose smiled. "But if you don't want to go with us, I understand; that's why I came looking for you alone. I thought maybe you didn't want to say anything in front of him."

The more Rose talked, the harder it was not to like her. Plus, Ethan's annoyingly kind girlfriend was right: paying for a cab would be a pain. And Alice wasn't exactly swimming in money at the moment. As for Uber, one tiny, money-forgetting-ATM-detouring incident last year had made her passenger score drop and now drivers ducked her requests.

Alice made up her mind. "I'm cool."

Ethan was waiting for them at the front of the house, now transformed into an unofficial parking lot. Luckily, they'd come in the pickup, so Alice wouldn't have to squeeze in the back of his sports car.

"You're still at the Botanic Gardens?" Ethan asked, catching her eye in the rearview mirror.

Alice blushed, thinking she'd had sex with him there, in her room. "Yeah, still there."

The awkward trio spent the ride in silence; each of them busy with their own thoughts. Alice didn't pay attention to the road, so when Ethan pulled up in front of her building, she was startled they'd already arrived. She was about to get out of the car when she froze, her hand on the door handle, her pulse out of control.

Jack was sitting on the steps of her building.

Forty-one

Alice

Spotting her, Jack sprang to his feet. "Hey," he said, jogging toward her. "Whose truck was that?" He frowned at the leaving car.

"Ethan's," Alice replied, not offering any further explanation.

Jack's face darkened. "Are you dating him again?"

Alice's shoulders slumped forward. "No." She was tired of playing games. "He and *his girlfriend* gave me a lift back from Georgiana's wedding. Madison and I went together in her car this morning, but she had some kind of crisis and left mid-party." Alice searched her clutch for her keys and headed toward the door. "I should probably check on her."

Jack trailed her. "Yeah, I saw her go inside."

Alice narrowed her eyes at him. "How long have you been waiting here?"

"Pretty much all day."

The admission jolted Alice's heart, but she decided to ignore it. "Did Madison look all right?"

"She wouldn't speak to me. But she had puffy eyes."

Alice made to insert the keys in the lock. "Then I should definitely go see if she's okay."

"Wait." Jack grabbed her elbow gently. "Can we talk, please?"

"It's been a long day," Alice protested. "And I can't stand on these heels any longer."

"Let's sit down then."

Jack pulled her away from the door and toward a nearby bench.

Alice let him at first but then chickened out. Jack ambushing her like this was too much. One ex in a day had been enough, and even if Jack wasn't officially an ex, it still felt that way. "I think I really should go check on Madison." She resisted his pull.

"Look," Jack said, peeking over her shoulder. "There goes another bridesmaid to take care of Madison."

Alice turned around. Victoria, Georgiana's sister, was ringing the bell to her apartment.

"How did you know she's a bridesmaid?" Alice asked.

"Same long, lavender dress as Madison." Jack shrugged. "It can't be that popular."

Alice's resolve not to talk to him softened. "I don't know if I should be scared you just used the word 'lavender' or not."

Jack shot her a grin—an interiors-melting one.

"Come on, Ice. We need to talk. And Haley's here, too." Jack jerked his chin at the building entrance. "Madison is taken care of."

Alice turned her head. Haley and Victoria were standing in front of the door, having some kind of argument. Alice finally gave in. With Haley there, Madison would be fine. She let Jack drag her the rest of the way to the bench.

Jack looked nervous and wasn't talking, so Alice prompted him. "What are you doing here?"

"You wouldn't take my calls."

Because the next time we talked, I'd have to say goodbye to you, Alice thought. Better get it over with quickly. "Okay, so what is it?"

"I came to apologize," Jack stated simply.

"For what?" Alice snapped. "For sleeping with my friend, for not telling me, or for something else?"

"All of it, and more."

Alice panicked. "I can't do this, Jack. I can't."

"Do what?"

"Have this conversation with you." He frowned. So Alice explained, "The 'we can't be friends anymore' conversation."

"Sorry, but we'll talk about how we're not going to be friends." Jack tapped a finger on his thigh. "Right now."

A crack spread through Alice's heart. "So you agree." She stared at the floor. "We can no longer be friends?"

"Is that what you want?" Jack asked. "To be my friend?"

She looked up at him. "No."

"Good, neither do I."

"And what do you want?"

Jack pinned her with his stare. "You, Ice. I want you."

Air escaped her lungs as she spiraled down a vortex of possibilities. Then fear kicked in. "Yeah, right," she said.

"Is it really that hard to believe?"

"The only time I tried to kiss you, you did everything you could to push me back. So, yeah, it is."

"You caught me off guard. I didn't expect it. I didn't know how to react." Jack gathered his thoughts. "I didn't even know how I felt, and by the time I had a good idea, you were already dating Peter."

"And now you know?" Alice asked, still skeptical.

He locked eyes with her and closed the space between them. "Yes."

"And how is that?"

Jack brushed the hair away from her face. "We're not *just* friends," he whispered, never lowering his gaze. "We never were."

Alice wasn't ready to accept these words. She'd waited too long to hear them. "And you realized this when?"

Jack looked at the sky in a way that said, "You're not going to make this easy for me."

No, she wasn't.

He trained his eyes back on hers. "I think I first realized it—subconsciously, at least—on umbrella night. When that dude grabbed you. When he pulled you away, and you struggled to get free but couldn't, I wanted to beat him into a pulp."

"That was a year ago," Alice noted.

"I know, but again from the first moment I saw you with Peter…" Jack made a strangled noise with his throat. "All I've wanted to do is smash his face. I've been rotting with jealousy ever since."

Could this be true? Was Jack really saying… *What was he saying?*

"Was the umbrella at Christmas…" Alice paused, appalled. Not sure what to ask. "Was it some sort of encrypted message I should've deciphered to… to what?"

"I didn't put that much thought into it. I saw a bunny-shaped umbrella, it reminded me of you, of that night, and I wanted to give it to you."

Alice narrowed her eyes at him. "Were you pretending to sleep on the plane the next day?" she asked, her voice daring him to deny it.

Jack frowned, a red flush creeping up his neck. "I had been waiting for a break ever since you started dating Peter. I couldn't wait to leave for Hawaii because I knew you and him wouldn't be together. That I wouldn't have to guard my shoulder in case I bumped into you two on campus, or change libraries because you were already there, *with him.*"

Alice stared at him, her mouth gaping open. That was exactly how she'd behaved around Jack's girlfriends all along. *Avoid. At. All. Costs.* Hope bloomed inside her chest.

"So, yeah," Jack continued. "When you told me you were coming along, I freaked out. I didn't want to deal with you and him on my trip. So I pretended I was sleeping."

"You said you were tired because you'd spent the night with someone," she accused.

Jack shook his head. "Peter said it, and I let everyone believe it." His shoulders sagged forward. "Because it was better than the alternative, than you learning the truth."

Alice raised her eyebrows in a silent interrogation.

"That I'd spent the night awake, dreading seeing you and Peter together every single day of the trip."

Alice tried to imagine what being on a trip with Jack and one of his girlfriends would do to her. *A slow death.* But, still, she couldn't let herself believe him. If she did, then… no, it would hurt too much.

"The night I met Peter," she said, ice in her voice, "you went home with Becky."

Jack didn't lower his gaze. "Ice, you want a list of all the stupid things I did?"

Alice nodded.

"If you promise to listen to everything else I have to say, I'll give it to you. Deal?"

"Deal."

Jack smiled, relieved, and took her hands in his. "From the moment I saw your lips stained blue, I hated Peter. *Hated* him. I wanted to be the one kissing you. But did I say so? No. I did what I do best and got drunk out of my mind and slept with the first girl I saw."

Jack talking about sex with other girls was like having an invisible hand wrap around her heart and have it suddenly squeeze. Alice bit back the bitter retort already forming on her lips and forced herself to remain silent. To listen.

"Then the next morning I woke up in her apartment," Jack said. The only emotion in his eyes was regret. "And she threw me out, and it felt... pointless. I was tired of being with people I didn't care about—"

Alice interrupted him by wrenching her hands free. They immediately felt too cold, and she wanted to put them back where they'd been. But Jack talking about the girls he'd slept with was making it hard for her to sit still and listen to him. She pinned him with a stare, asking, "So you haven't slept with anyone since—what, October?"

"No," he replied, unflinching.

Alice's eyes widened. "Don't mock me, Jack. You expect me to believe you've gone"—she counted on her fingers—"seven *months* without sleeping with anyone?"

"No one since Becky."

There wasn't a trace of hesitation in his voice or features. A little smile spread on Alice's lips, and she couldn't stop it. "Go on," she said. "With the list of stupid things you did."

Jack reclaimed her hands. "Umbrella night, I wanted to kiss you." A black hole opened where her stomach should've been. "And that day at the library," Jack continued, "the same. But I was scared of history repeating itself, like what happened with Felicity, and I couldn't bear to lose you the same way I lost her. *Not you.* So I pushed you away and spent an hour taking a freezing shower; not that it did me any good. Then at the party you acted as if nothing had happened, you pushed your friend on me, and you kissed Peter."

Alice felt the need to admit some of her own stupid actions. "I was trying to make you jealous."

"It worked." Jack flashed her a mischievous grin. "After your first date with Peter, I lost my mind. I was even more stupid."

"How?"

"I told you not to date him because he was bad for you. And when that didn't work, I tried to have him hook up with some random girl to prove my point and make you ditch him."

Alice couldn't stop the foolish smile tugging at the corners of her mouth from spreading, or the small fire that was now burning in her chest. "You're really bad," she said.

"I am, was." Jack squeezed her hands. "My next tactic was to ignore you, and him. To pretend you didn't exist, or that the two of you weren't together."

Alice knew that particular tactic all too well; she'd used it many times on him.

"Then there was Hawaii, and I couldn't fool myself anymore," Jack said. "So I pretended to sleep to avoid you. That night, when I saw Peter come into your room—"

"You saw that?" Alice asked, shocked. A furious blush invaded her face. "How?"

"My room was directly opposite to yours. David and Scott Williams fighting was the best thing that happened in Hawaii. When I saw you head back to your room with Haley, I was happy. I was glad two of my teammates had almost beaten each other to death if it meant you got to spend one less night with Peter."

Alice's mind was exploding. "Why didn't you say anything?"

Jack scoffed. "Coming from you, that's rich."

Alice pulled her hands away from his grip again and stood up. "Excuse me?"

Jack sprang up from the bench and was in her face in a blink, crowding her. "You say you've known for years, so why didn't *you* say something sooner?"

"I tried." She glared at him. "You rejected me."

"And you claimed to have been on the rebound."

"Are you saying you believed me?"

"No," Jack admitted. "I never said anything after that day because you were with Peter. It didn't seem right."

"And trying to have him sleep with other girls was right?"

"That was a week into your relationship. You hadn't slept with him yet. When you became steady, it seemed wrong to try to break you two apart. I didn't want to hurt you." Jack paused. "And when you broke up, I messed up again."

"Madison," Alice whispered. That invisible hand was back at her heart and squeezing. "Was that another one of the stupid things you did?"

"Not telling you was stupid. And, yes, it was deliberate." For once, Jack was owning it. "Have you ever wondered why I never as much as looked at someone in our concentration, or at one of your close friends—"

"You slept with Becky."

"You pushed her on me," Jack protested. "And she's not a close friend."

"And why were close friends and people in our concentration off-limits?"

"Ice, you know why. It felt like crossing a line," Jack explained. "One I crossed with Madison, but only because I didn't know you'd meet her in the future and become best friends."

"And why didn't you cross that line, knowingly?"

"To leave the door open."

"The door to what?"

"You and me."

"Jack, you're contradicting yourself every five seconds. First, you didn't know. Then, you've always known… None of this makes sense." Alice took a step back. "I'm too tired for this. I'm going inside."

Jack grabbed her by the shoulders gently, keeping her in place. "No, you're not," he said. His tone was final. "I know I'm not making much sense, but I've come to tell you something, and you need to hear me say it."

Alice's heart was beating too fast. She couldn't speak.

Jack's right hand traveled from her shoulder to her neck, ending up buried deep in her hair. "I love you, Ice. And I'm not afraid. I won't be stupid again and not kiss you. Even if it is just this once." His other hand moved down to her lower back, and he pulled her close to him. The hand at the back of her nape tilted her head upward, and Jack's lips brushed against hers.

Alice's knees buckled. She wrapped her arms around his neck for support, her fingers slipping through his dark hair. A million times she'd imagined kissing Jack, but none of her fantasies could have prepared her for the real thing. Everything inside her melted. All her fears, all her insecurities, all the pain and jealousy. It was all gone, obliterated by this kiss.

Jack broke the kiss. "I love you," he whispered.

"I lo—" Before Alice could say it back, he was kissing her again, and this time her knees really did give way.

Jack scooped her up into his arms and began to carry her away from her building.

"Where are you taking me?" Alice asked, losing herself in his eyes.

"Home. With me. And I'm never letting you go ever again. Deal?" Jack flashed her that mischievous grin she loved so much.

Alice beamed back at him. "Deal."

To Be Continued…

Note from the Author

Dear Reader,

I hope you enjoyed *Friend Zone.* If you loved or hated my story **please leave a review** on Goodreads, your favorite retailer's website, or wherever you like to post reviews (your blog, your Facebook wall, your bedroom wall, in a text to your best friend...). Reviews are the biggest gift you can give to an author, and word of mouth is the most powerful means of book discovery. It helps readers find new authors they love and it helps the authors *you* love stand out.

Book three in the series, *My Best Friend's Boyfriend*, will focus on Madison, Haley and, *yes,* those Williams brother. Alice and Jack will be there, too, as will most of the characters from the first book. I hope you'll want to keep following them on their journey.

Turn the page for a very short teaser from *My Best Friend's Boyfriend.*

Thank you for your support!
Camilla, x

Sneak Peek - My Best Friend's Boyfriend

One

Haley

Now

"I don't have an umbrella," Haley called, having to shout to be heard over the rumbling summer storm. "Do you?"

"No," David yelled back. "And I don't care."

He hurried past her out of the cover of the library porch and ran down the steps. When he reached the bottom, he tilted his face up and closed his eyes. In a matter of seconds, he was soaked.

"What are you doing?"

David looked at her from across the street, he was walking backward toward the center of Harvard Yard. "Come here. It's only water."

Haley didn't know what possessed her, but she did as he asked. She ran off the porch and joined him in the middle of the park. The sensation of the rain on her skin was electrifying as she spun on her toes, arms opened wide. Haley looked upward and laughed and laughed, unable to stop—until she pirouetted right into David's arms. The smile died on her lips as he caught her wrists and held her hands close to his chest, leaning his head down…

She tried to pull back, a ragged breath catching in her throat. "David, don't."

David's lips brushed her forehead in a soft, wet kiss. "I wasn't going to," he whispered. "The next time we kiss, you'll want to just as much as I do now…"

Sneak Peek: My Best Friend's Boyfriend

One

Haley

Now

Acknowledgments

The first huge thank you goes to my street team. I've only just created this group a few months ago and your support has already been overwhelming.

Thank you to all readers. Without your constant support, I wouldn't keep pushing through the blank pages. Thank you to my editors Hayley Stone and Michelle Proulx for making my writing the best it could be.

To my family and friends for your constant encouragement.

Acknowledgments

[illegible]

[illegible]

[illegible]

Made in United States
North Haven, CT
26 June 2022